D0458342

MR. LEMONCELLO
AND THE
TITANIUM
TICKET

PLAY ALL THE GAMES, SOLVE ALL THE PUZZLES— READ ALL THE LEMONCELLOS!

ESCAPE FROM MR. LEMONCELLO'S LIBRARY

MR. LEMONCELLO'S LIBRARY OLYMPICS

MR. LEMONCELLO'S GREAT LIBRARY RACE

MR. LEMONCELLO'S ALL-STAR BREAKOUT GAME

MR. LEMONCELLO AND THE TITANIUM TICKET

CHRIS GRABENSTEIN

This is a work of fiction. Names, characters, places, and incidents either are the product of the author's imagination or are used fictitiously. Any resemblance to actual persons, living or dead, events, or locales is entirely coincidental.

Published in the United States by Random House Children's Books,
a division of Penguin Random House LLC, New York.

Random House and the colophon are registered trademarks
of Penguin Random House LLC.

Visit us on the Web! rhcbooks.com

Educators and librarians, for a variety of teaching tools, visit us at
RHTeachersLibrarians.com

Library of Congress Cataloging-in-Publication Data
Names: Grabenstein, Chris, author.
Title: Mr. Lemoncello and the titanium ticket / Chris Grabenstein.
Description: First edition. | New York: Random House Children's Books, [2020]
| Series: Mr. Lemoncello's library; book 5 | Audience: Ages 8–12.
Summary: "Four lucky kids go on a scavenger hunt inside Mr. Lemoncello's Gameworks factory, where they compete for a chance to win a Titanium Ticket"
—Provided by publisher.
Identifiers: LCCN 2019031138 | ISBN 978-0-525-64774-4 (hardcover) |
ISBN 978-0-525-64775-1 (lib. bdg.) | ISBN 978-0-593-18144-7 (int'l) |
ISBN 978-0-525-64776-8 (ebook)
Subjects: CYAC: Treasure hunt (Game)—Fiction. | Contests—Fiction. |
Libraries—Fiction. | Books and reading—Fiction. | Eccentrics and
eccentricities—Fiction. | Friendship—Fiction.
Classification: LCC PZ7.G7487 Mc 2020 | DDC [Fic]—dc23

Printed in the United States of America
10 9 8 7 6 5 4 3 2 1
First Edition

Random House Children's Books
supports the First Amendment and celebrates the right to read.

FOR THE PARKER BROTHERS,
THE HASSENFELD BROTHERS (HASBRO),
AND MILTON BRADLEY:
THANKS FOR MAKING GROWING UP SO MUCH GIGGLY FUN.

"There goes that clock again!" said Akimi Hughes as, off in the distance, four musical notes chimed three separate times. "We only have fifteen minutes left. Hurry!"

"I'm hurrying!" said Kyle Keeley.

"Hurry faster."

Kyle and Akimi had traveled from their homes in Ohio to help the world-famous game maker Mr. Luigi L. Lemoncello test out a brand-new, supersecret interactive gaming experience that would soon have its gala grand opening in Hudson Hills, New York—a town Kyle and Akimi had always dreamed of visiting.

Because Hudson Hills was where Mr. Lemoncello made all his games!

During the day, they'd toured the unbelievably amazing factory and eaten peanut butter pie with marshmallow and chocolate sauce in the company cafeteria. Tonight, they'd spent two hours running around inside a mysterious world of puzzles, games, and holographic surprises—piecing together a cryptic message on a tablet computer.

"Here comes our final riddle," said Kyle.

A string of letters scrolled across the video screen in the dashboard of the miniature amusement-park car they were sitting in.

"Oh, joy," said Akimi. "This only makes, what? Eight of 'em?"

Kyle glanced down at the tablet's screen. He and Akimi needed to enter their response to the riddle in a series of letter bubbles, spaced to represent words, just like in the game hangman. Some of the bubbles had numbers underneath them.

○○ ○ ○○○○○○○○ ○○○○
25 13 50 16 70

"Okay," said Kyle, "this is going to be a four-word answer. Two letters, one letter, eight letters, four letters."

"This is also the most complicated game Mr. Lemoncello ever created!" said Akimi.

"Because the prize is huge," said Kyle. "A titanium ticket! Titanium's better than gold, right?"

"Totally," said Akimi.

"But what's it a ticket *for*?" wondered Kyle.

"Something bigger than big, or Mr. Lemoncello wouldn't've flown us here on his private jet to test it!"

"You're right! Okay. Here's our riddle: 'When can you jump over three men without getting up?' "

"Duh. Easy," said Akimi. " 'In a checkers game.' Two letters, one letter, eight letters, four letters. Ka-boom!"

Kyle tapped in Akimi's answer. The letters in the numbered bubbles automatically appeared in the corresponding numbered spaces in the phrase that Kyle and Akimi had been slowly piecing together as they worked their way through eight different game stations.

"Excellent," said Kyle, watching the computer do its thing and slide the numbered letters into the appropriate positions. " 'I' is going to twenty-five, 'N' to thirteen, 'C' to fifty . . ."

"Um, Kyle? I can see the screen. I don't need a play-by-play."

Kyle and Akimi had been best friends forever—even before they started winning all sorts of games together inside Mr. Lemoncello's library, back home in Ohio. But a ticking time clock could strain even the tightest of friendships. Right now, they were a guitar string—one tuning-peg twist away from snapping.

The tablet computer blared a triumphant, if tinny, trumpet fanfare.

"Yes!" said Kyle. "With that answer, we have officially filled in the whole phrase."

Kyle and Akimi climbed out of the cramped little red car they had successfully maneuvered through a massive traffic jam of brightly colored vehicles that had blocked them in. A soothing female voice purred from hidden ceiling speakers: "Congratulations, KYLE and AKIMI. You have successfully completed all eight games."

"Yes!" said Kyle, with an arm pump.

"Booyah!" added Akimi, slapping him a high five.

"Good luck with the rest of your quest," said the recorded voice. "We hope you make it to the finals."

Kyle and Akimi stared at each other.

Finally, Akimi exploded. "The rest of our quest? We're not done? We filled in the whole phrase!"

"What 'finals' is she talking about?" added Kyle.

"You have seven minutes remaining," cooed the calm voice.

"To do what?" Akimi shouted at the ceiling.

Kyle's mind was spinning. Racing. "Maybe there's a hidden code in the phrase." He looked back at the game screen. "Hang on." Sixteen letters in the final phrase started glowing, the circles behind them turning into fluorescent-yellow lemons.

"We've got glowing letters," he reported. "G-E-C-E-C-D-E-D-C-D-G-D-C-E-G. And another 'G.' "

"You think it's some kind of anagram?" asked Akimi.

"Maybe," said Kyle. "We should figure out all the words we can make with those sixteen letters."

"Good idea! Um, 'deeded,' " said Akimi. " 'Ceded,' 'edged,' 'egg' . . ."

"Egg!" said Kyle. "Mr. Lemoncello probably hid an Easter egg somewhere in one of these rooms."

"Easter was a while ago, Kyle. The egg would be rotten by now. We would've smelled it."

"In video games, an Easter egg isn't a real egg; it's an inside joke," he explained. "A hidden message . . ."

Akimi looked around. "Oh. So how do we find it?"

"I have no idea."

"Wait!" said Akimi. "Maybe it's a substitution code, where every letter stands for a different letter! Mr. Lemoncello has done that before."

"You're right! But we need some sort of clue to know how many letters to skip ahead in the alphabet."

Akimi snapped her fingers. "There's a license plate on the back of this car!"

She scurried around to the rear bumper.

"What's the number?" asked Kyle.

"Three!"

Kyle tried to think faster than fast. "Okay, we jump ahead three letters in the alphabet."

"Or we could count three backward," said Akimi. "After all, this is the *rear* bumper!"

"Let's do forward first."

"Fine."

Kyle started at the beginning of the string of glowing letters.

" 'J' is three letters past 'G' . . ."

“‘E’ becomes ‘H,’” said Akimi. “‘C’ becomes ‘F’ . . .”

“And ‘D’ becomes ‘G’!” added Kyle.

“So,” wondered Akimi, “does that mean ‘D’ becomes ‘J,’ too? Because if ‘D’ is ‘G’ and ‘G’ is ‘J’ . . .”

“Why are there only four different letters?” shouted Kyle. “Why aren’t any of them vowels?”

“‘E’ used to be a vowel!” Akimi shouted back. “Until you made me turn it into an ‘H’!”

“You’re the one who did that!” countered Kyle.

“Because you told me to! I knew we should’ve gone backward!”

Off in the distance, clock chimes played their hourly melody and started tolling.

It was nine o’clock.

“Sorry,” said the voice in the ceiling. “Your quest remains incomplete. You lose.”

“We lost?” Kyle groaned.

“Only because *this is impossible!*” screamed Akimi.

Suddenly, she heard a series of familiar, high-pitched burp-squeaks. A hologram of Mr. Lemoncello, dressed all in black except for his bright-yellow banana shoes, stepped out of the shadows.

“Impossible?” he said. “Oh, it’s possible. But for a prize this humongous, I’m afraid the final puzzle must be magnifficult: which is to say, magnificently difficult! Because whosoever solves it will automatically win a titanium ticket and move on to the final round!”

"The final round of what, sir?" Kyle asked politely. He'd loved Mr. Lemoncello since forever, but sometimes . . .

"Sorry," the hologram replied with a sly wink. "I can't tell you. Not yet, anyway. For, you see, good friends, the final round will be the most important game ever played in the history of gaming! Because the winner will become an instant bazillionaire!"

It was after nine o'clock on a school night.

Simon Skrindle, a short (and nearly invisible) seventh grader at Hudson Hills Middle School, had just crept out of the dark forest near the Lemoncello Gameworks Factory.

He was a twelve-year-old on a mission.

He was alone. Simon didn't have many friends, especially not the kind who'd go on an adventure with him, sneaking through the woods late at night.

And this was a BIG adventure.

Simon was going to be the first to see what secrets were hidden inside the new building *behind* Mr. Lemoncello's factory!

For twenty-five years, Luigi L. Lemoncello, the world-famous game maker, had manufactured his games inside the fantastical castle fortress of the Lemoncello

Gameworks—a sprawling factory perched high on a hilltop overlooking the Hudson River. Its four corner towers looked like upside-down snow cones made out of lemon-yellow oval bricks. The pinnacles at their pointy tips were topped with cello weather vanes. Sculptures of game pieces served as gargoyles. The factory's water tower was a one-million-gallon lemon on stilts. During the day, enormous smokestacks puffed out billowy clouds of steam in the shapes of animals or famous faces. Simon loved seeing the Abraham Lincoln and George Washington clouds drifting across the sky over the factory every Presidents' Day. And the bunnies at Easter time. People came from all over to take selfies with the cartoon clouds. Another pipe let out enormous rainbow-colored bubbles every weekend.

There was also a giant ball-pit moat surrounding the whole factory and you could only enter when the drawbridge was lowered. Workers had to know the secret password and shout it into an enormous curled horn that looked like something out of a Dr. Seuss book.

And for the past five years, Mr. Lemoncello had spent a ton of money and time constructing a top-secret new building close to his factory fortress. All the work had been done behind forty-foot-tall plywood walls (painted yellow, of course). The workers and contractors and architects had been sworn to secrecy about what they were doing on the other side of that wooden barricade.

Rumors buzzed around the town, anyway.

One guy at school, Jack McClintock, whose dad was the head of security at the Gameworks Factory, said the new building was nothing but a fancy warehouse for "storing junk." A girl in Simon's science class, Soraiya Mitchell, whose father was the plant manager, said the new building would be filled with "amazing twenty-second-century game-making technology."

Basically, nobody knew what was inside the new building. But everybody wanted to find out. Kids at school were even daring each other to "bust in."

No one had the nerve to try.

Then, two weeks ago, the yellow plywood walls came down to reveal a modern, three-story silver box with mirrored walls. At night, those walls reflected back the twinkling black sky.

Plywood down, the secret glass building was now surrounded by three rings of chain-link fences, set up in concentric circles. Each fence had a locked gate, which could be reached by following a footpath from the factory parking lot past a bed of yellow and orange flowers spelling out the word "gesundheit," then on through rows of topiary—evergreen shrubs trimmed to resemble Mr. Lemoncello in various poses (juggling, dancing, tipping an egg timer, balancing a pair of giant dice on his nose). Some kids at school said the fences were electrified, too.

Security for the new building was tight. Super tight.

Simon's grandfather, who hated all things Lemoncello, swore that "the batty old bazillionaire is installing an army of robots in that new building so he can fire all the factory workers!"

Simon's grandpa, Sam Skrindle, had no proof for his theory. It was more or less a wild guess.

That's all anybody in Hudson Hills had. Wild guesses and theories based on even wilder rumors.

So Simon decided *he* would be the first one to actually step foot inside Mr. Lemoncello's secret new building. He'd show the kids at school. He'd take their dare. He'd also take a few pictures with his phone to prove that he'd done it.

Besides, Simon had what his grandmother called "an insatiable curiosity." He loved tearing things apart just to see how they worked. And then he loved putting them back together.

Usually, he could.

Except that one time with his grandmother's blow-dryer. When Simon put it back together, the thing sucked air *in* instead of blowing it *out*. It inhaled her hair like a hungry, hungry hippo slurping spaghetti.

It took a week for the bathroom not to smell like a charred wig.

Fortunately, his grandmother wasn't upset. She laughed and said, "Yep, just like your father."

Simon's grandparents were some of the few adults in the whole town who had never, ever worked at the Gameworks Factory. Mr. Lemoncello was the main employer in Hudson Hills. Had been for twenty-five years. Everybody said he paid the best wages in the world and had the best benefits, too—medical, dental, free books, a rock climbing wall, two zero-gravity rooms, plus an indoor archery range *and* a bowling alley.

Everybody in Hudson Hills loved the zany game maker.

Everybody except Simon's grandfather, who said the meanest, nastiest, ugliest things about Mr. Lemoncello—at the grocery store, at the hardware store, at the barbershop, in letters to the local newspaper, even after church on Sundays.

Sam Skrindle was the town kook.

Maybe that's why Simon didn't have very many friends.

And why he had to break into the secret building!

If he did, he'd prove to all the kids at school that not everybody in Hudson Hills named Skrindle was a total joke.

Simon scurried across the moonlit lawn, past a topiary trimmed to look like Mr. Lemoncello floss dancing, and made it to the pathway, which he followed to the first of the three locked gates.

There was a small metal box mounted on it. Inside the box, Simon discovered a thumbprint scanner, a video screen, and a keypad. He figured the scanner was for authorized workers. Everybody else probably needed to tap in some kind of security code to open the lock.

A recorded voice said, "Greetings and salutations!"

It was Mr. Lemoncello himself!

Mr. Lemoncello didn't visit Hudson Hills all that much, but Simon recognized his voice from TV commercials and the *All-Star Breakout Game* on the Kidzapalooza Network.

"To enter this supersecret zone," the recorded voice continued, "puzzletastic skills must be shown!"

A riddle scrolled across the video screen: *There are 100 bricks on a plane. One falls off. How many are left?*

Simon thought about that. He wondered if it was a trick question. *It couldn't be this easy.* Then he shrugged and tapped *99* on the keypad.

A flashing *Correct!* filled the screen and dissolved into animated fireworks. The pixels rearranged themselves to create a new question: *What are the three steps for putting an elephant into a refrigerator?*

What? Simon thought. He knew Mr. Lemoncello was wacky, but this question was just plain weird.

"It'd have to be a jumbo-sized fridge," he mumbled. Then he thought out the logical steps. *One, open the door. Two, put the elephant in. Three, close the door.* It made sense, so he typed those three steps on the keypad.

"Oh, what fun!" boomed Mr. Lemoncello's recorded voice. "You have opened lock number one!"

There was a solid *CLUNK* of a latch springing free. The gate creaked open an inch. Simon pushed it the rest of the way and hurried down the yellow brick walkway to the second gate, where he found a second puzzle box.

Another question glowed on its screen: *What are the four steps for putting a giraffe in a refrigerator?*

Simon started to type in the same answer that he'd just given for the elephant/fridge question.

Then he stopped.

That was three steps. This question asked for four.

He needed an extra step. He rubbed the short, fuzzy

hair on top of his head as if it were a lucky tennis ball. Sometimes head rubbing helped him think. So did humming.

What if it's the same refrigerator? he asked himself. He shrugged again. He took a risk and typed in his answer, even though it felt more like a guess: *One, open the door. Two, take the elephant out. Three, put the giraffe in. Four, close the door.*

The screen remained frozen for a second.

Then it burst into those *Correct!* fireworks again.

The dots pulled themselves together to form another question: *A lion was having a party and he invited the other animals. All of them came except one. Which one was it?*

"How should I know?" muttered Simon. "There are so many animals in the jungle. . . ."

He heard a whir overhead.

It was a security camera, swiveling slightly on its post. One more swivel, and its lens would be aimed directly at Simon.

Panicking, he typed the first and only thing to cross his mind: *The giraffe*. Simon figured it couldn't come to the lion's party because it was stuck in the refrigerator.

He closed his eyes and hit the enter key.

"Well, yippee-ki-yay and husker dü!" cried Mr. Lemoncello's voice. "You have unlocked gate number two!"

The second gate popped open. Simon couldn't believe his luck. He raced to the third and final gate just before the overhead security camera completed its pivot to catch him. He was so close to the building, he could see his reflection in the mirrored glass walls. He flipped up the lid on the lockbox and read the riddle he knew would be waiting for him: *A lady crossed a crocodile-infested river and survived. How?*

This question seemed to have nothing to do with any of the earlier ones. Maybe Simon's grandfather was right. Maybe Luigi L. Lemoncello was just a madman with a mangy mustache.

Or . . .

Maybe the new question *did* have something to do with the old ones.

Simon's fingers danced across the keypad. *There weren't any crocodiles in the river,* he typed. *They were all at the lion's party.*

He was correct. Again.

Two words illuminated the screen: *Final Question.*

This was it. If Simon answered one more question correctly, he'd be in. He'd be the first unauthorized person in all of Hudson Hills to see what was inside the new top-secret building!

Up came the final puzzler: *The lady waded back across the river and died. How?*

Simon's cranium felt like it might explode.

The crocodiles could've left the party early. The river could've turned into quicksand. There really weren't enough facts to work with.

Or were there?

Maybe *all* the riddles were connected!

Maybe the final answer would come from that ridiculously easy first question.

Simon took a deep breath. He was ready to play his hunch.

The brick from the airplane fell out of the sky and conked her on the head, he tapped on the keypad.

"Congratulicitations to thee!" the prerecorded Mr. Lemoncello declared. "You have solved the riddles for gate number three."

Simon didn't hear the familiar metallic *CLUNK* of the lock opening.

He pushed against the gate. The chain-link fence rattled but the gate didn't budge.

"You made it oh so far," the voice continued. "So be oh so proud. However, access to the general public is not yet allowed. Thank you for playing. Your memories are your treasures. It's time for me to activate maximum security measures!"

Freaking out just a little, Simon jiggled the third gate again.

It still wouldn't open. He heard the double *KA-THUNK* and *WHOOSH* of what sounded like a pair of catapults.

FWUMP!

Direct hit.

Ew!

The hurling machine had clobbered Simon with some kind of flying beef potpie loaded with gravy, potatoes, and slimy meat chunks.

He heard something creaking overhead. Looking up, he saw two rubber buckets perched on top of the gate's tallest posts. The teetering tubs were hooked up to a gears-and-pulleys contraption. The kind of thing Simon loved making. The buckets were starting to tilt.

Simon thought about running.

He probably should've just done it.

Because, while he stood there thinking about it, the buckets dumped their loads directly on his head.

SCHWUMP! SPLAT! BANG!

Greasy gravy and bacon sludge flattened his hair and dribbled down the back of his shirt. It was extremely gross. And smelly.

From off in the darkness, Simon heard barking. Lots of yips and yaps and happy squeals.

Mr. Lemoncello had released the hounds!

And Simon Skrindle was standing there frozen. A meat-flavored Popsicle.

The factory's guard dogs would tear him to shreds.

He ran to the gate behind him.

It had relocked itself. Simon tugged. The gate clattered. But there was no escape. He was trapped. Looking right and looking left, he could see the sharp-edged silhouettes of charging dogs.

They seemed to be small.

Angry Chihuahuas with sharp, pointy teeth? Beagles trained to hunt foxes? Miniature hounds and jackals?

No.

As the twin dog packs drew closer, Simon could see that they were all puppies. Floppy-footed, tail-wagging, head-bobbing, ear-flapping puppies.

Dozens of them. Maybe a hundred.

They leapt up and toppled Simon to the ground so he'd be easier to lick.

Two puppy tongues lashed the insides of Simon's ears while six others nuzzled his armpits and another two burrowed under his cuffs and tried to scoot up the legs of his pants. Simon giggled and squirmed. The dogs were so snuggly and squiggly he couldn't help it.

A sharp whistle pierced the night.

"Here, Sounder, Ginger Pye, Old Yeller, Winn-Dixie, and all you others I haven't had time to name yet!" cried Mr. Lemoncello's voice through the outdoor loudspeakers. "Your job is done. Here at the Gameworks Factory, security is always fun!"

The puppies hopped off Simon and, tails wagging, waddled away.

On what had to be the weirdest night of his life, Simon heard the catapults fire again.

This time, they lobbed a pair of fluffy, lemon-scented beach towels over the fence.

Simon stood up, grabbed the towels, and started cleaning what was left of the meaty slop (not to mention gobs of dog drool) off his face, hair, and clothes.

Behind him, he heard the third gate squeak open. Simon braced himself. He figured the real security guards were coming out to arrest him.

To Simon's surprise, he saw Kyle Keeley and Akimi Hughes. They were the famous kids from Mr. Lemoncello's holiday commercials. The ones who won the escape game at Mr. Lemoncello's library in Ohio.

"Hi," said Kyle while Akimi locked the gate behind them. "Good job on those riddles. It's like Mr. Lemoncello always says: The future belongs to the puzzle solvers."

Simon raised his hand.

"Question?" said Akimi.

"Uh, yeah," said Simon. "What are you two doing here?"

"Mr. Lemoncello asked us to beta test his newest creation," said Kyle, jabbing a thumb over his shoulder to indicate the secret building.

"What is it?" asked Simon. "What's inside?"

"Sorry, Simon," said Akimi. "That information is classified."

"At least until this weekend," added Kyle with a wink.

Simon heard the second and then the first gates *CLICK* open.

"Catch you later, Simon," said Kyle. He and Akimi headed toward a car shaped like a cat that had just silently prowled into the parking lot.

"Wait a second," Simon called after them. "How did you know my name?"

Kyle turned around and smiled. "Mr. Lemoncello told us. He's been watching you. He's a big fan."

Simon was confused. "Of what?"

Akimi laughed. "You, Simon Skrindle!"

Jack McClintock's father was the head of security for the Lemoncello Gameworks Factory.

He had been for eleven months.

That meant Jack was basically his number one deputy.

The McClintocks lived in a house on the Gameworks property. The guardhouse had been built to resemble a gingerbread house, complete with gumdrop shrubs and candy cane gutters. Thanks to Mr. Lemoncello's patented smell-a-vision indoor air fresheners, the whole house smelled like gingersnaps.

Jack's dad thought the house was ridiculous. Jack did, too. A seventh grader at Hudson Hills Middle, Jack liked to go to school wearing camouflage. Or all black. All black was good, too. Made him look like a ninja. Or a member of a SWAT team.

In addition to a regular TV, the McClintocks had a

special room filled with five dozen small video monitors—one for each security camera surveilling the Gameworks Factory and grounds. There were another five dozen blank ones on the opposite wall. They'd cover the insides of the new secret building once it became operational.

Jack's father had only been working for Lemoncello for a short time and didn't really like how the bazillionaire ran his factory. Especially its security.

"Too loosey-goosey for my taste," he'd say. "If this were my factory, I'd lock it up tighter than a drum. Then I'd do deep background checks on all employees."

Jack wasn't a big fan of the "world's greatest" game maker, either, because, in his opinion, Mr. Lemoncello didn't have enough first-person shooter games. Those were Jack's favorite.

But, a job was a job and, according to Jack's dad, this one came with great benefits, not to mention free rent, which was good, even if you had to live in a house with oversized M&M's for doorknobs.

So, when an alarm sounded anywhere on the factory property, day or night, the McClintocks, father and son, sprang into action!

"Scramble, scramble!" Jack's father hollered up the staircase. "We need to be Oscar Mike!"

Security personnel everywhere knew that meant "on the move."

Jack rolled away from his homework desk and plucked his tactical jacket off the back of his chair.

"Intruder alert?" he shouted down the steps.

"Roger that!" his dad hollered back. "Interloper at the gates. Grab your moonbeam."

That meant "flashlight." Jack had no idea why. Neither did his dad. It was just another thing, like Oscar Mike, that they said in the Marines. Jack's father was never a Marine but he always wished he had been.

"Do you two need a snack?" asked Jack's mom as he and his dad raced through the kitchen. She started spreading peanut butter across slices of white bread.

"Negatory," they both replied.

"We have a kid sneaking around the new building," said Mr. McClintock. "Can you ID him, Jack?"

He showed Jack a screenshot he'd taken with his phone.

"Ten-four, sir," said Jack. "That's Simon Skrindle. Total I-D ten-T."

Mr. McClintock nodded. He understood the code: I-D 10-T. According to Jack, Skrindle was an idiot.

"He's the class joke, sir," Jack continued. "A total waste of space."

"He's a dummy?" asked Mr. McClintock, arching a skeptical eyebrow. "Then how'd he make it through the first two gates and successfully complete the riddles for the third?"

"He got lucky, sir."

Jack had tried to answer the riddles of the gates himself. He'd wiped out at the second gate. Mr. Lemoncello's guard puppies had licked him mercilessly.

"Let's roll," said Jack's father. "We need to go nab your friend. His time's up!"

"He's not my friend, Dad!"

They ran out the back door, leapt over the mini-pretzel fencing, and headed to a small shed. Jack's father reached inside and shoved up a large lever. A blindingly bright spotlight thumped on.

Jack saw Simon Skrindle standing outside the fence line, looking like a scared raccoon caught with his paws in a dumpster.

"Freeze!" shouted Jack's father.

"You heard my dad!" shouted Jack. "Freeze!"

Skrindle obeyed their commands. He even put his hands up over his head.

"Don't shoot!" he cried.

"At ease, son," said Jack's dad. "We don't carry weapons. That's against Mr. Lemoncello's rules—unfortunately. Are you Simon Skrindle?"

"Yes, sir."

"Wait a second," said Jack's dad. "Are you related to Sam Skrindle? The grouchy old coot who's always bad-mouthing Mr. Lemoncello around town?"

"Yes, sir. He's, uh, my grandfather."

"What were you doing back here?" asked Jack's father.

"Nothing, sir," replied Simon.

"You're good at that," cracked Jack.

Jack's father hiked up his utility belt. "Tell you what, Simon. I'm gonna let you go. This time. Having to be Sam

Skrindle's grandson seems like punishment enough. You are free to return home. But don't you ever try to break in again or you'll have a real soup sandwich on your hands."

"Yes, sir. I won't, sir."

Jack and his father watched Simon Skrindle scurry off toward the woods.

Despite what he'd said to his dad, Jack couldn't help but marvel a little.

How did that little squirt figure out all six riddles?

At school the next morning, everybody was buzzing about that weekend's big company picnic and town-wide celebration.

Posters were hung in the hallways promising "A Major, Earth-Shattering, Moon-Blasting, Mars-Jiggling Announcement to Be Made by Mr. Luigi L. Lemoncello Himself!"

That meant Mr. Lemoncello was coming to the company picnic.

"The twenty-fifth anniversary is the silver anniversary!" Simon heard one kid say. "Mr. Lemoncello will probably give everybody a commemorative silver coin!"

"No way," said another. "That would be boring. This is going to be something awesome!"

"I bet he's going to open up the secret building!" said a third kid. "After all, those mirrored walls are kind of silvery!"

Simon wished his grandfather hadn't outlawed all things Lemoncello. The twenty-fifth annual company picnic, with all its games and surprises, sounded like fun. But Simon had never been to one.

At lunch, Simon sat by himself in the cafeteria. He was only two tables away from where Jack McClintock sat with his usual crew. Jack was wearing a green, brown, and tan camouflage T-shirt and olive-drab cargo pants. The camouflage didn't really make him disappear or blend in with his surroundings. It made him look like a tree eating a cheeseburger.

"I picked up some major intel this morning," Simon heard Jack say to a kid at his table. Jack had a very loud voice. "This weekend, after the picnic, four kids are going to be the first ones to see what's inside the new building."

"No way!" said one of his buds.

"Way. You have to earn your way in by being a top finisher in the sidewalk board game, which they say is going to be more like an incredible obstacle course this year."

"Cool!"

"But—you don't make it to *that* unless you win a bunch of preliminary games in the carnival tents first."

"You'll do good at those, Jack. You crush all those Lemoncello riddles. You're like a mastermind!"

"Guess it comes from living out at the factory," said Jack.

"Hey, Jack," said another guy at the table. "Have you

ever tried to sneak in? Get a peek at what's going on back there?"

"Negatory. It'd be a waste of time. Mr. Lemoncello has rigged up a series of lockboxes that are tougher to crack than any combination or code."

"How come?"

"You have to answer *six* riddles. Two at each of the three gates. And the riddles? Trust me, guys—they are impossible to solve. The toughest ones Mr. Lemoncello has ever come up with."

Simon couldn't help but grin.

He'd answered all six!

After lunch, Simon had a free period in the library. He was working, by himself, in the maker space, putting the finishing touches on a towering, six-foot-tall K'nex and Lego Ferris wheel.

He'd used over 8,550 different pieces. The wheel would turn thanks to a motor Simon had improvised out of Circuit Cubes. Carnival music would be supplied by a recycled MP3 player linked to the motor's on-off switch. There was a pneumatic tube elevator that shot action-figure passengers straddling a Ping-Pong ball up to the top of the Ferris wheel.

Simon had been working on the project every day for two weeks, encouraged by Mrs. Jill Merkle, the school librarian. She was the one who helped Simon find the bits and pieces he needed to make his idea leap to life—including some tiny finger puppets she had from her days as an elementary school librarian. The miniature people would ride in the cars of Simon's wheel.

"You know," Mrs. Merkle told Simon, "this is exactly how Mr. Lemoncello got started."

"Really?"

"Oh, yes. When he was your age, he used to go to his local public library, where the librarian would let him tinker with his ideas. She even lent him things out of her desk drawer, like a Barbie doll boot. That's why there's a boot token in his Family Frenzy board game."

"Cool."

"Very. You ready to give your wheel a whirl?"

"Just about. I need to snap together a few final circuits."

"Well, let me know before you flip the switch. I want to be here for the grand opening. Maybe shoot a video."

Mrs. Merkle bustled off to see what all the noise and commotion was on the other side of the carrels separating the maker space from the rest of the library.

Simon soon found out.

It was Jack McClintock, wearing a pair of Lemoncello Virtual Reality Goggles. He came stumbling into the maker space, blindly swinging a pool noodle.

"Jack?" said Mrs. Merkle. "Put that down."

Jack remained oblivious. He was wearing noise-reducing headphones, too.

"This is so cool!" he shouted. "There's a castle. And dungeons. And dragons!"

"Jack?" Mrs. Merkle tried again.

But behind the goggles, Jack couldn't see what his virtual sword was about to do in the non-virtual world.

He gave the pool noodle a swing, and Simon's view of the coming disaster seemed to shift into slow motion.

Nooooooo! cried a panicked voice inside his head.

Mrs. Merkle's hands flew up to her head as her eyes bugged out.

Jack's foam stick smacked the side of Simon's Ferris wheel. His masterpiece exploded. Eight thousand, five hundred and fifty different pieces went flying.

When Jack finally heard all the plastic clattering, clinking, and skittering across the floor, he tipped up his VR goggles, took off his headphones, and surveyed the scene.

"Hooah!" he said. "Awesome. I slayed the dragon *and* whatever Skrindle was playing with! I should earn bonus points for that."

"No," said Mrs. Merkle. "You should earn a detention! Come with me, Mr. McClintock."

She led Jack to her desk.

Simon didn't say a word.

Inside, he was furious. Outside? He kept quiet, and after mourning the ruins of his two-week project for a moment, he started cleaning up the mess.

Simon Skrindle hadn't been dealt the best cards in the game of life.

Both of his parents had passed away when he was an infant.

"Tragic accident in Asia" was the only thing his grandfather ever told him about the particulars. His grandmother would just get weepy.

After school, Simon trudged up the front porch steps of his grandparents' two-story frame house on Oak Street. He checked out the newspaper-retrieving gizmo he'd rigged up on the front lawn. It was basically a little red wagon that Simon had repurposed with grooved cog wheels that could roll on slanted rails elevated over the stoop's five steps.

When a newspaper landed in the bed of the wagon, its weight depressed a swivel pad, which released a bungee cord attached to an anchor hook sunk into the lawn. That caused a counterweight attached to a cable on the porch (it weighed one pound more than the wagon with a full Sunday newspaper in it) to slide downhill into the yard, pulling the wagon up its elevated railroad.

That way, his grandmother didn't have to walk through the wet grass every morning in her slippers to retrieve the local paper.

The one Grandpa Sam sent all his angry letters to.

"Welcome home, Simon," said his grandma when he hung his backpack on a peg in the foyer. She gave him a kiss on his forehead.

"Hey, Grandma."

"How was school?"

"Fine."

"Well, fine is better than bad, I suppose. Oh, Simon, I've been meaning to ask you: Can you please take a look at the shelf thingamajig in the kitchen cabinet over the sink? It stopped working this morning."

Simon had rigged up motorized shelves in the kitchen cupboards using some display cases he'd found in a dumpster behind the downtown jewelry store. With a flip of a switch, the shelves in the front would glide down while the shelves in the back slid up. Bringing the shelves to eye level made it easier for Grandma to find what she was looking for without climbing a ladder. (Grandma was almost as short as Simon.)

"The drive chains probably slipped out of their sprockets," said Simon, flipping out the screwdriver head on his Swiss Army knife and heading into the kitchen. "I'll fix it."

"Thank you, dear."

Grandpa Sam was sitting at the kitchen table, watching a tiny black-and-white TV. The local news station was doing a story about the "big Lemoncello company picnic, which will feature a major announcement from Mr. Lemoncello himself. Something about a titanium ticket . . ."

Grandpa Sam snapped off the TV.

"You need to fix this TV next," he grumbled at Simon.

"Okay, Grandpa. What's wrong with it?"

"It keeps talking about Mr. Lemoncello!"

Simon had a bedroom on the second floor, but his favorite place in the creaky old house was up in the attic.

That was his lab. His very own "imagination station."

The attic was always hot but Simon didn't mind. You had to climb a drop-down ladder to get up there—something his grandparents, with their various aching joints, didn't want to do. Simon had outfitted the ladder mechanism with a remote-controlled Clapper someone had thrown out, so the steps automatically unfolded and lowered whenever he clapped his hands three quick times. (He also said, "Open sesame," but that was just for fun.)

Simon had the whole attic to himself, including a dirt-streaked circular window tucked into an angled dormer. From that secret observation post, three stories up, he could watch other kids playing in their yards or doing chores or climbing into their family cars for a trip to . . . somewhere. Anywhere.

Simon imagined going with them. He'd make up stories about the exotic places they were visiting, what they saw, and the incredibly fun things they did.

Since Lemoncello (and all other) games were banned in his home (Grandpa thought games were a waste of time), Simon made up his own board games in the attic. Sometimes, he used brightly painted stones for playing pieces. Other times, secondhand action figures he bought at neighborhood yard sales or found in curbside trash bins on recycling day. That's where Simon also found things to tear apart and put back together. Clocks (he particularly liked cuckoo clocks). Remote-controlled cars. A rainbow-colored glockenspiel with the notes written on the thick wooden keys.

Simon didn't tear the wooden xylophone apart when he found it on sale for twenty-five cents at a garage sale. But since it was missing its mallets, he had to improvise a new pair. He did it with two rods and a pair of round connectors from a Tinkertoy set a six-year-old two streets over had tossed to the curb when she turned seven.

Music helped Simon think. He'd sit down, plink out a simple melody on the color-coded keys, and daydream. Einstein had his violin to help him do thought experiments. Simon had a toy glockenspiel.

Simon had also heard that Mr. Lemoncello did his best thinking while tooting on a tuba.

That made Simon smile. A lot of the stuff he heard about Mr. Lemoncello (his banana shoes, his head phone, his hover slippers) made Simon smile.

He just made sure that Grandpa Sam didn't see him doing it.

The next day at school, Simon sat at his usual lab desk in science class: the one at the back, near the smelly chemical storage closet.

The one where no one else ever sat.

He was doodling in his notebook, working out his plans for a mega Lego wall project for the library. Mrs. Merkle said he could have the space for a week. Simon wanted to turn the bright-green wall into a sideways board game with pathways, obstacles, and challenges. He'd use Lego characters as the playing pieces.

Jack McClintock swaggered into the science lab with a bunch of his friends.

"Check it out, bros," he said, pulling a rubber-banded stack of four-by-six note cards out of his backpack. "My dad made me some flash cards."

"For what?" asked one of his friends. "Algebra?"

"Negatory. These are to help me get ready for the qualifying games at the picnic. Drill me!"

One of his friends held up the first flash card. Because Simon was behind Jack, he could see what was printed on it:

LEAF
LEAF **CL**
LEAF
LEAF

"Um, Leif Eriksson," said Jack. "That Norse explorer dude from Iceland."

"Nope," said his friend, checking the answer scribbled on the back of the flash card. "But 'leaf' is one of the words. . . ."

"Well, duh," said Jack. "It's printed like four times on the card. Uh, how about 'Leaf me alone'?"

"Sorry, dude," said Jack's friend.

"Try again," urged another.

While Jack stared at the card, Simon wrote the answer on his doodle pad: *Four-leaf clover.*

"Skip that one," said Jack. "It's impossible. Nobody could answer it."

"Okay," said his friend, discarding the first puzzler. "The answer was four-leaf clover."

Simon grinned.

"Give me the next one," ordered Jack.

His friend flicked up a second flash card:

WORDS
FUNNY WORDS
FUNNY WORDS
WORDS

"Okay," said Jack, thinking hard. "Two funnies. Four words . . ."

"Correct!" said his friend.

"Huh?"

"Too funny for words."

"Exactly," said Jack. "That's what I said. Too funny for words. Just like Doofus McGoofus in the back row." He jerked his chin at Simon.

Simon ducked his head and circled the *too funny for words* he'd scrawled on his doodle sheet.

"Give me one more," said Jack. "And make it a tough one!"

His friend flashed him a third card.

WBOEOADRS

"Okay," said Jack. "That's just a mess."

"Want me to tell you the answer?" asked his friend. "It's on the back of the card."

"Negatory!" said Jack. "It's a jumble. I can make

all sorts of words with those letters. We. Boards. Boo. Robo . . ."

"Um, that's not the answer," said his friend.

Simon wrote down his answer, covering it with his hand so no one could see it: *A bear in the woods.*

Meanwhile, Jack was still unscrambling words from the letters.

"Beard! Woods. Bear. Bear in the woods!"

"Correct!" shouted his friend. "Awesome, man."

"Thanks. It's because I live out at the factory. I just sort of soak the answers into my brain through mental osmosis."

The science teacher, Mrs. Allison Bickhardt (the kids all called her Mrs. Big Heart), came into the room.

"Good afternoon," she said, rubbing her hands together eagerly. "Are you psyched for our field trip?"

Simon had forgotten. Today was the day his class was supposed to go see all the amazing science, technology, and engineering behind Mr. Lemoncello's Gameworks Factory. Soraiya Mitchell, who always got 100s on everything, had arranged the special "backstage tour" because her father was the plant manager.

But Simon had known his grandfather would never sign a permission slip for him to go on a field trip to anywhere connected with Mr. Lemoncello. And Simon didn't want his grandmother signing it, either, because if she did, Grandpa would get all cranky. So Simon hadn't even bothered asking. He figured he'd just spend the rest of the day in the library, working on his Lego wall creation.

"Here you go," whispered Soraiya, who always sat at the lab table next to his. She handed Simon a folded sheet of paper.

Simon was confused. "Um, what is this?"

"Your permission slip."

"But my grandparents didn't sign . . ."

"Yes, they did," Soraiya said with a smile. "I told them they had to sign a receipt for all the free Girl Scout cookies I gave them this morning."

"So," Soraiya said to Simon ten minutes later, as the school bus they were riding in lumbered up the road to the Game works Factory, "I've decided you and I should be friends."

"Really?"

"Yep. We're both puzzle solvers. I like the intellectual kind. You're more practical. You build stuff."

Simon and Soraiya were seated next to each other in the second-to-last row.

"I saw that Ferris wheel you were working on in the library," said Soraiya. "Why'd you take it down?"

"There was an, uh, accident."

"Really? Was the accident named Jack McClintock?"

"Yeah."

Soraiya shook her head. "You should just try to avoid him. It's like Einstein supposedly said: 'Stay away from negative people. They have a problem for every solution.'

Oh, I saw that newspaper retrieval system you engineered in your front yard when I dropped by with the Girl Scout cookies. Totally awesome."

"Thanks. How'd you know where I live?"

"I used the scientific method."

"Huh?"

"You know. Research. Data."

Simon nodded. Slowly.

Soraiya laughed. "I looked up your address in the school directory."

"Oh. Right."

"My dad said it was very important that you come to the factory today."

"Why?"

"I don't know. I have a few hypotheses but I need to gather more data before I reach a conclusion."

The bus rumbled through a pair of tall wrought iron gates that seemed to magically swing open as the bus drew near.

"Wow," said Simon.

"Motion detectors," said Soraiya, with a shrug. "Passive infrared sensors. The bus entered their field and triggered the switch to an electric gate-opening motor."

"Look at all those cool carvings in the iron! I see a boot, a cat, a top hat, a roller skate, a penguin, a dinosaur . . ."

"Those are all the playing pieces from Mr. Lemoncello's very first game, Family Frenzy."

As the bus pulled closer to the factory, colored plumes of smoke shot up, creating a daytime fireworks display. The cellos atop the lemony turrets bowed themselves and played a beautiful melody that Simon recognized. Steam pipes shot up a puffy cumulus cloud that looked exactly like Mrs. Bickhardt, the science teacher. Chains rattled and the drawbridge to the front entrance started to creak down.

"Looks like they knew we were coming!" said Mrs. Bickhardt, admiring her floating cloud. The bus eased to a stop. "Come on, you guys. It's tour time! And I need to grab a selfie!"

At the far end of the bridge, which spanned the ball-pit moat, a jolly man in a bright-yellow jumpsuit and a hard hat resembling half a lemon stepped through the factory's twenty-foot-tall front doors that had been intricately carved to resemble two sideways labyrinths. A pair of shimmering brass cheese wedges tucked into angled corners of the mazes served as doorknobs.

"Whoa," Simon whispered. The factory was even more impressive in daylight.

"Welcome, welcome, welcome!" boomed the jolly man.

"That's my dad," said Soraiya. "He can be a little over the top. Especially on field trip days."

"Behind these doors," Mr. Mitchell said dramatically, "is where science, technology, engineering, art, math, and fun go to work every day. So, of course, do many of your parents, grandparents, aunts, and uncles!"

Not mine, thought Simon.

"Hello there, Soraiya!" Mr. Mitchell gave her a fingertip-waggling wave.

"Hey, Dad."

"Thank you again for arranging this tour, Mr. Mitchell," said Mrs. Bickhardt. "And for my cloud."

"My pleasure. I'm happy to show you and your students everything I can."

"How about the secret building out back?" shouted one of Jack McClintock's buddies.

"Sorry. No can do."

"What's in there?" asked Mrs. Bickhardt.

"No one knows," said Mr. Mitchell. "Except, of course, Mr. Lemoncello and his top-secret team of engineers, architects, and construction workers. It's been quite an operation. Most of the work was done at night, after the factory was closed."

"When can we go in?" shouted a girl named Augusta Westhoff. "When's the new building going to be open?"

"This weekend!" announced Mr. Mitchell. "Right after the company picnic and outdoor board game!"

"Woo-hoo!" shouted everybody who'd been on the bus.

"But only for four children," said Mr. Mitchell. "The ones competing for the titanium ticket. Now then, are you folks ready to cross the bridge and step inside?"

"Yes!" shouted the entire class.

"Then someone shout 'jubjub jabberwock' into the horn! That's the special visitor password this week."

Augusta ran to the horn, which looked like what Dr. Seuss called a floofloover, and said the magic words. The towering wooden doors behind Mr. Mitchell groaned open.

Simon looked down into the ball-pit moat. About a dozen people were mirroring the moves of an instructor, doing exercises that pushed and shoved the balls into rippling piles.

"That's this morning's ball-pit aerobics class!" Mr. Mitchell had to shout to be heard over the throbbing salsa music booming behind him. "Let's head inside, kids! And, if you see a family member, be sure to signal for a drone camera to fly over and snap a selfie."

"Technically," Soraiya whispered to Simon, "it's not a selfie if a floating drone takes the picture for you."

"Right. But it still sounds pretty cool."

"True. You don't have any family on the inside, do you?"

"No," said Simon. "My grandfather is, you know, retired."

"But this isn't your first time inside the factory."

"Huh?"

"Nothing. Just something my dad said this morning over breakfast."

"You guys talked about me?"

"Little bit. Then we came up with that permission slip–Girl Scout cookies scenario. My father is very clever."

"This way, children!" cried Mr. Mitchell.

He ushered the science class into the building before Simon could ask Soraiya any more questions.

And the instant Simon saw what was inside the factory, he was too amazed to ask anybody anything.

Simon couldn't believe what he was seeing.

The place was huge! It was fantastic! It was amazing!

Workers, all of them in yellow jumpsuits and lemon wedge hard hats, danced to piped-in salsa music as they pressed buttons, cranked levers, and stomped on foot pedals that made high-tech printing presses roll, card cutters slice, plastic coating drums whirl, and shrink-wrappers swirl.

Mr. Mitchell passed out half-lemon hard hats for all the visitors. Some of Simon's classmates found family members and posed for the camera drones darting around snapping souvenir photographs.

"Factory work can be monotonous," Mr. Mitchell explained over the din of the machines and the music's pulsing beat. "So, to make it more fun, we do it to music. Today is Latin day. Tomorrow? Country swing! Putting games together is like doing a dance. Each step leads to the next step. Everything must be done in a logical, synchronized routine."

"Dancing is such a waste of time," Simon heard Jack mutter to one of his friends. "My dad would make such a better plant manager than that joke Mr. Mitchell. . . ."

"Do you come up with the ideas for the games?" asked Augusta.

"No," said Mr. Mitchell. "Mr. Lemoncello and the other game makers dream up the ideas down at the Imagination Factory offices in New York City. Up here? We make them real—and put them in a box. That's what engineering is all about, folks. Turning dreams into reality!"

"What game are you working on today?" asked Augusta, who always asked the most questions in science class.

"Mr. Lemoncello's Loony Loop-de-Looper," said Mr. Mitchell. "It's a knitting game where you win plastic pearls. First one to string together a necklace wins! Today, we're molding millions of miniature pearl beads, which is why we need to refill the injection tanks!"

He pointed toward the fifty-foot-high ceiling, where two workers strapped into hover packs floated near a white silo and fed pellets of plastic into a hopper at the top.

"The tower, wrapped with heating coils, will gently melt the plastic as a corkscrewing plunger presses it down to be injected into the pearl molds."

Simon couldn't resist. He raised his hand.

"Question?" asked Mr. Mitchell.

"Yes, sir. Since heat rises, wouldn't it be more energy efficient if the heating tube were horizontal instead of vertical? If it were horizontal, both ends would be the same temperature and you'd get even melting."

"What a dumb idea," snorted Jack.

Mr. Mitchell stroked his chin, thinking about what Simon had said. He was about to answer when Augusta blurted, "What's this?" She pointed to a huge high-tech device that looked like an upside-down plastic octopus trapped inside a big white box.

"That, my friends, is a three-D body scanner. You stand in that center circle and the one hundred twenty-eight cameras in those eight panels will capture a three-hundred-sixty-degree image of you."

"What's it for?" Augusta always had a lot of questions.

Mr. Mitchell's eyes twinkled. "Who'd like to become a game piece today?"

Everyone shot up their hands.

"Then line up! We'll capture your image and send it to our three-D printer!"

While everybody else waited for their 3-D scan, Simon and Soraiya wandered over to a printing press to watch sheets of game boards rolling out of the mechanical contraption.

"I would love to take that machine apart," said Simon.

"Could you put it back together?" asked Soraiya.

"I think so."

"You want to line up to do the three-D game-piece thing with everybody else?"

"No thanks," said Simon. "I just want to watch these machines. They're amazing!"

Soraiya had spent a lot of time inside the factory with her dad. She showed Simon everything. The card shuffler. The plastic wrapper. Even the 3-D printing machine.

"Why, look," said Soraiya as the machine spun plastic strands to build a miniature, one-inch-tall Jack McClintock token. "He's not so big and tough anymore!"

After about thirty minutes of marveling at the machinery, Simon and Soraiya joined the rest of their class in the gift shop.

"Hearty and splendiferous greetings to you all!"

Simon looked up.

Mr. Lemoncello was hovering near the ceiling.

Well, it was a holographic projection of Mr. Lemoncello, but it was extremely realistic.

Simon felt like he could pluck the tiddlywinks buttons right off his checkerboard vest.

Mr. Lemoncello doffed his top hat and tossed it to the floor, where it landed with a loud, metallic clunk.

"Yes, here at the Lemoncello Gameworks Factory, everybody, including me, must wear a hard hat. Mine's made out of steel. I hope you enjoyed your tour today."

"We did!" said Augusta. "It was awesometastic, sir."

The holographic Mr. Lemoncello smiled and bounced up and down on the heels of his banana shoes, nodding to the left and then to the right, as if more visitors were heaping praise on him and his factory. Simon figured he must have a preprogrammed wait time whenever he pretended to be interactive.

"Sorry. I wasn't pretending to be interactive. I was thinking about this year's brand-new sidewalk board game, where the top four finishers will— Drumroll, please . . ."

A holographic bass drum rolled across the floor, chased by a holographic drum major in a tall, puffy hat.

Mr. Lemoncello picked up where he left off: "The top four finishers will be the first to see what's inside my new, supersecret building!"

"Hooah!" shouted Jack.

"Here are the rules—for what would a game be without rules, except cardboard, shrink-wrap, and plastic playing pieces injected vertically into a mold when everybody knows doing it horizontally would be much more efficient."

What? thought Simon. *Did Mr. Lemoncello somehow hear my comment back on the factory floor?*

"Now then, what was I blathering about? Ah, yes. The rules! To qualify for the outdoor board game, you must first play three preliminary games in the tents that will be set up on the picnic grounds. The top finishers in those games will move on to our all-new, superslimy Slippery-Sloppery Sidewalk Board Game. The top four finishers there will become the first four visitors to my new and amazingly incredible building, where, in our third competition of the day, you might find a titanium ticket that will . . ."

Mr. Lemoncello froze. Simon leaned forward.

"Oops. I almost gave it away. I hate when I almost do that."

Mr. Lemoncello bent down, grunted, and with a herculean effort hoisted his heavy metal top hat off the floor. He slowly lowered it to his head, but the heavy hat slammed down hard and wobbled like a manhole cover. A circle of chirp-chirping bluebirds swirled around his head.

"Oooh. I'm feeling dizzier than usual. My hair feels rustier, too. It's time for me to depart. Toodle-oo, everybody. I look forward to seeing you all this Saturday at the biggest, messiest, and bestest company picnic ever!"

Mr. Lemoncello snapped his fingers and disappeared in a holographic *poof!*

"He is so awesome!" gushed Augusta.

"He's a nutjob," grunted Jack.

"All right, class," said Mrs. Bickhardt. "Let's head back to the bus."

As Simon's classmates filed out of the factory, someone tapped him on the shoulder. It was Mr. Mitchell. He was holding a crisp envelope with a waxy yellow seal stamped with a scrolled letter "L."

"Mr. Lemoncello asked me to give you this. The *real* Mr. Lemoncello."

World-famous librarian Dr. Yanina Zinchenko was touring the secret new building with Mr. Chester Raymo, Mr. Lemoncello's head imagineer.

Dr. Zinchenko's red hair swayed with every stride as she clicked her way up a shadowy corridor in her jazzy high-heeled shoes, which, of course, were also red. Mr. Raymo, who was dressed in his frumpy white lab coat, tried his best to keep up with her. It wasn't working. He was at least three steps behind as they walked down a corridor.

"This is not a library," Dr. Zinchenko said in her thick Russian accent. "Nothing is organized as it should be. I think Mr. Lemoncello has invented a new cataloging concept: the Screwy decimal system."

"You are correct, Yanina," said Mr. Raymo, who was a little short of breath. "This is not a library. However, it has been no trivial pursuit, either. This the most technologically advanced building Mr. Lemoncello has ever created. He hopes it will, one day, become his legacy!"

"It's too early for Mr. Lemoncello to be thinking about legacies," said Dr. Zinchenko.

"Perhaps," said Mr. Raymo. "But none of us is getting any younger. And the future belongs . . ."

Dr. Zinchenko finished the thought for him. "To the puzzle solvers. Da, da. I have heard Mr. Lemoncello say this many, many times."

They entered the building's vast atrium, where the focal point was a towering grandfather clock featuring figurines of a fantastical array of children playing games. The carved characters stood frozen, ready to spring into motion at the stroke of the hour.

The walls were covered with framed art. Three dozen holographic projectors were fastened to a grid under the fifty-foot ceiling. Clear tubes, illuminated by colorful LEDs, snaked their way through the empty space overhead. Pathways led out of the atrium to what could best be described as an indoor amusement park filled with fun and games. Lots and lots of games.

"It is time to plant the prize in the designated position," said Mr. Raymo. "May I please have the titanium ticket, Yanina?"

He held out his hand.

Dr. Zinchenko sighed and handed Mr. Raymo the slender slip of shiny metal. "Do what needs to be done, Mr. Raymo."

Mr. Raymo slipped the thin metal rectangle into its hiding place.

"It's for the future, Dr. Zinchenko," he said, rather ruefully. "The future."

"Da, da. So everybody keeps telling me. Come along. I am feeling sad and blue. I need to see some books! Books make me happy."

"Right this way," said Mr. Raymo, leading her out of the atrium and into a room where the walls were lined with bookcases.

"Ah!" said Dr. Zinchenko, craning her head to take in the beauty of the leather-bound volumes. "This is, as Mr. Lemoncello might say, wondermous."

"Indeed," said Mr. Raymo. "I believe this collection contains every book, magazine, and scholarly article ever written about board games. I suppose the children who visit won't spend much time in here."

"Of course not," said Dr. Zinchenko. "They'll be too busy exploring all the gizmos, gadgets, and games! Especially the—"

Dr. Zinchenko's high-tech earpiece began to buzz. She tapped it to answer.

"Yes?" she said. "Very well, Mr. McClintock. We'll be right there. Give us five minutes."

"Trouble?" asked Mr. Raymo.

"No. Just our pre-picnic security meeting. We should use this swirly slide to expedite our exit."

"Oh, joyyyyyyyyyy."

* * *

Dr. Zinchenko and Mr. Raymo hurried through the security gates (making sure they were locked tight behind them) and made their way to Mr. McClintock's office in the gingerbread house. (Mr. Raymo wanted to take a bite of the giant jelly bean door knocker. Dr. Zinchenko advised him it was actually made out of aluminum.)

"Welcome to our pre-picnic PPC meeting," said Mr. McClintock as he opened the door.

Dr. Zinchenko arched an eyebrow above her sparkly cat-eye glasses. "A P-P P-P-C meeting?"

"Roger that, ma'am," said Mr. McClintock, hiking up his pants, leading the way into the command and control center. "Potential party crashers. Bad actors who might try to sneak into town this weekend and gum things up. You ask me, we should beef up security. Eliminate some of the more frivolous activities that could provide cover for uninvited intruders. That's what I would do if it were my factory."

"What did Polo Orozco, head of security at the Imagination Factory in New York, tell you?" asked Mr. Raymo, who didn't seem interested in what Mr. McClintock would do if this were his factory.

Mr. McClintock bristled a little. He knew when he was being cut off.

"Mr. Orozco advises me that all Chiltingtons are accounted for. None of them are headed to Hudson Hills."

"Good," said Dr. Zinchenko. "And Mr. Lemoncello's

primary competitors in the domestic toy and game market, the Krinkle brothers?"

"They are attending a pachisi conference in Palm Springs."

"Excellent. Thank you, Mr. McClintock. Keep up the good work. Please keep in constant contact with Mr. Orozco. We must not allow anything to ruin this weekend's celebration."

After school, Simon showed his grandmother the wax-sealed envelope Mr. Mitchell had given him.

"Oh, my," she said. "That 'L' is lovely."

"It's from Mr. Lemoncello," Simon whispered.

His grandmother nodded. "Go upstairs and open it, Simon," she said with a gentle smile. "I'll make your grandfather some soup. Keep him busy in the kitchen."

"Thanks, Grandma."

"Shh," she said. "This will be our little secret."

She eased herself out of her chair and toddled off to the kitchen.

Simon headed up to his room. He closed the door, and after rubbing the bumpy "L" in the yellow wax seal with his thumb a few more times, he carefully pried the envelope open.

Inside was an engraved invitation from Luigi L. Lemoncello himself.

HEARTY AND SPLENDIFEROUS SALUTATIONS!

MASTER SIMON SKRINDLE,
YOU ARE HEREBY AND FORTHWITH
(NOT TO MENTION FIFTHWITH)
INVITED TO PARTICIPATE IN THE GAMES
AND GENERAL SHENANIGANS AT MY
TWENTY-FIFTH ANNIVERSARY
GAMEWORKS COMPANY PICNIC,
EVEN THOUGH NOBODY IN YOUR FAMILY CURRENTLY
WORKS THERE.
SEE YOU ON SATURDAY.
AND, YES, THERE WILL BE BALLOONS.

WARMLY, BECAUSE MY AIR CONDITIONER IS BROKEN,
LUIGI L. LEMONCELLO

* * *

That Friday at school, just about everybody was buzzing about the big event or drilling themselves on Lemoncello-style puzzles. They all wanted to be one of the first four kids to see what was inside the new building and maybe win the titanium ticket (even though nobody knew what it was a ticket to).

"Last year, the picnic was so awesome!" Simon heard people say. "This year, it'll be even more amazing! The new sidewalk board game sounds lit! And Mr. Lemoncello is coming to town!"

Some kids in the cafeteria were rolling dice and chasing each other around board games. Others were playing Lemoncello video games on their devices. Over at his table, Jack McClintock was having his buddies flash him more rebus cards.

"Hit me again!" Jack shouted.

Up came the new card.

THINK U SPEAK

"Think before you speak!" said Jack. "Next one."

**LITTLE LITTLE
LATE LATE**

"Too little, too late!"

"Correct again," said his friend. "Dude, you are on a roll."

"I've been practicing. Let's just do one more. Don't want to wear myself out. Need to save something for tomorrow . . ."

"Good strategy. Here you go. Last puzzle."

Jack stared at the card. For like ten seconds.

STANDS

0_23456789

Simon scribbled his answer in his notebook.

"It's some kind of math problem," he heard Jack mutter.

"It's okay if you can't solve it, Jack," said his friend. "The label on the back says this one is a black diamond. That means it's extremely difficult."

"Probably because no one understands it."

"Correct!" shouted his friend. "There's no 'one' under 'stands.' No one understands! Jack, you are a genius. A genuine genius."

Jack looked confused for a second. But he snapped out of it pretty quickly. "Yeah. I'm good. But I still can't crack that riddle Ms. Pulliam put up on the board."

Ms. Elizabeth Pulliam, who taught math, was always challenging her classes with riddles and puzzles.

"Nobody else could solve it, either," said his friend.

Curious as usual, Simon strolled down the hall to Ms. Pulliam's room while everyone else finished lunch. He stepped into the empty classroom and read what Ms. Pulliam had posted on her bulletin board with a question mark magnet:

Two fathers and two sons sat down to eat eggs for breakfast.
They ate exactly three eggs.
Each person ate only one egg. How?

Simon grinned. He knew the answer.

It was actually kind of simple.

Since the room was empty, and nobody could see him doing it, he wrote his answer on a yellow sticky note from a pad he found on Ms. Pulliam's desk:

One of the fathers is also a grandfather.
His son is the father of the other son.

Simon stuck his answer on the board, right underneath the riddle.

And then he actually giggled.

Solving puzzles? It was a blast.

Simon woke up early on Saturday morning and reread his engraved invitation from Mr. Lemoncello—for the fifteenth time.

Did every kid in town get one? he wondered.

Probably not. Most of their parents worked at the factory. They were automatically invited to the picnic. He tucked the thick card into the back pocket of his jeans and made his way down to the kitchen.

His grandmother was already there, waiting for him.

"I know breakfast is the most important meal of the day," she whispered, "but I think you should skip it this morning, Simon. Your grandfather is sound asleep. Go grab your bike and head over to the park, honey. The company picnic is always an all-day affair. They'll have lots of food. I remember the one time we went."

"You went to a Lemoncello company picnic?"

She nodded. "That was a long time ago. . . ."

Her eyes teared up.

"Are you okay, Grandma?"

"Yes, dear. Just my allergies. Go on now. Have fun." She held open the back door. "Try not to make too much noise until you're down at the corner. Your grandfather needs his beauty sleep."

Simon nodded and tiptoed down the back steps. He jumped on his bicycle and coasted out of the driveway. He pedaled as quietly as he could until he reached the corner. That's when he started pumping his legs hard, racing over to Riverview Park, an eight-acre green strip between the Hudson River and the town's small downtown district.

As he got closer, Simon could see a crowd already starting to assemble near a sea of colorful tents and pop-up pavilions. Even though it was early morning, he could smell popcorn, roasted peanuts, and flash-fried funnel cakes. It was as if the circus and the county fair had both come to town on the same day.

Simon leaned his bike against a rack where some kids he recognized from school were stowing their bikes, too.

"Yo, did you hear about Jack McClintock?" said one.

"Yeah," said the other. "He cracked Ms. Pulliam's riddle. One of the fathers was also a grandfather. His son was the father of the other son."

"Jack's a genius!"

"Totally. Come on. We need to go check in."

The two guys took off running.

Simon jogged behind them. *Of course Jack McClintock copied my answer off that sticky note, which he probably tossed in the trash,* he thought. *He's not a real puzzle solver. He just memorizes answers.*

A cool shadow fell over Simon. Something had just blocked out the sharply angled morning sun.

Simon looked up.

A bright-yellow hot-air balloon was descending from the sky. It was shaped like a giant, floating lemon! The real Mr. Lemoncello, not a hologram, was riding in its gondola basket, waving his top hat at the cheering crowd.

"Halloo!" Mr. Lemoncello cried out. "It's so splendiferously delightful to be back here in Hudson Hills. Now, if you'll kindly clear a space, I need to land this hot-air balloon before I run out of hot air, which, according to anyone who has ever heard me speak in public, is virtually impossible. Stand back. I'm tossing over a sandbag! *Oopsy.* That was my *sandwich* bag. Peanut butter and banana! Here comes the sandbag."

Simon heard a loud *THUD,* followed by a sloppy *SQUISH.*

"Oh, my. The sandbag landed on top of the sandwich bag. Guess I'll be eating mashed bananas for lunch. Again!"

Simon made his way into the crowd circling Mr. Lemoncello's landing site. Since he was short, he was able to worm his way to the front just as the hot-air balloon touched down.

Simon had never seen Mr. Lemoncello in person—just on TV and in that hologram at the factory. Now he was only ten feet away! Simon thought he might faint. Especially when the genius game maker whirled around and looked straight at him. His coal-black eyes were twinkling.

"Ah, halloo there, young fellow. Could you kindly tie off this line?"

Mr. Lemoncello tossed Simon a coiled rope.

"I've got that," said Soraiya's dad, coming over to take the rope out of Simon's hands. "You need to go register for the games, Simon."

"Exactamundo!" cried Mr. Lemoncello from his balloon basket, where he was busily signing autographs for eager fans. "What on earth—or, for that matter, Pluto—are you waiting for, Simon? An engraved invitation? Oh. Right. If I'm not mistaken, you already have one! Go!"

Moving fast—as if somebody (or something) else were in charge of his legs—Simon chugged into the registration tent.

Where he bumped into a thick wall of eager kids.

There were four bunched-up lines totaling maybe three hundred gamers. The lines snaked up to cafeteria-sized folding tables where volunteers from the Gameworks Factory sat with clipboards and stacks of numbered bibs for the contestants to wear.

"Once you're registered," said the lady with a megaphone who seemed to be in charge, "you can play any three games you choose in the preliminary rounds. The top scorers from those rounds will move on to the Slippery-Sloppery Sidewalk Board Game on Main Street. That contest will start at two o'clock sharp. And you'll need to wear plastic jumpsuits or you'll ruin your clothes.

The top four finishers in that event will be the first to see what's inside Mr. Lemoncello's top-secret new building behind the factory, where they'll have a chance to win a titanium ticket!"

Everybody inside the tent applauded.

Simon's line shuffled forward.

When it did, he found himself standing side by side with Jack McClintock, whose line wasn't budging.

"What are *you* doing here?" asked Jack. "These aren't the lines for the porta-potties!"

His clump of friends laughed.

Jack narrowed his eyes into a squint. "You're not actually thinking about signing up for the games, are you?"

"Maybe," said Simon, without adding, *After all, Mr. Lemoncello did personally invite me.*

"Did you hear that, guys? The town clown thinks he can play games with top-gun gunners like us."

"Ha! Let him try," said one of Jack's friends. He was wearing a black T-shirt with skulls and crossbones printed all over it. "We'll crush him."

"These preliminary rounds are for serious gamers only," Jack told Simon. "You should go home and play with your blocks. Why embarrass yourself? Everyone knows you're a joke—just like your crackpot grandfather!"

Simon's line started moving again while Jack's remained stuck.

"Quit now, Skrindle, or you'll regret it later!" Jack shouted as Simon inched forward.

The only thing I might regret, thought Simon, *would be losing to you!*

Finally, he made it to the sign-up table.

"Hi there," said a friendly man with a name tag that ID'd him as Alex Renzulli from shipping and receiving. "Ready to play some games?"

"Yes, sir," Simon told Mr. Renzulli.

"Okeydoke. Just fill in the blanks and sign your name." He slid a clipboard across the table. Simon wrote down his name, address, and date of birth, then signed his name.

He slid the clipboard back to Mr. Renzulli.

"Fantabulous," said Mr. Renzulli. "You are number one-six-six. Pin this to the front of your shirt. Your scorecard is tucked inside the plastic pocket on the back of the bib."

"Okay. Thanks."

"And don't forget to grab a brochure. It lists all your options. They're all jumbo-sized versions of Lemoncello games, most of them made right here in Hudson Hills. We've got everything from Incredibly Kooky Kujenga to Three-D Thingama-Jigsaw Puzzlerama. Pick any three."

"Thank you, Mr. Renzulli," said Simon.

"My pleasure, Simon. Truly. My pleasure."

Simon stepped away from the table, opened the glossy pamphlet, and studied his options.

"Hey, Simon!" It was Soraiya. "You made it!"

"Yeah," said Simon, shyly tapping the square of plasticky paper pinned to his T-shirt. "I'm number one-six-six."

"I'm number one. Dad had to get here early to help set up. What game do you want to play first?"

Simon glanced down at the brochure.

He didn't recognize any of the Lemoncello games on the list because his grandfather wouldn't allow any of them in the house.

So he shrugged. "I don't know. What do you want to play first?"

Soraiya grabbed his hand. "Come on. I know something you'll be great at! Me too!"

"Incredibly Kooky Kujenga is Mr. Lemoncello's take on the Tumbling Tower–type game," Soraiya explained as they entered the game's tent.

"Sounds awesome," said Simon.

"It is. But Mr. Lemoncello doesn't use solid wooden planks in his version. That wouldn't be wacky enough. He substitutes wobbly gummy blocks. And since this is a jumbo version of the game, today those blocks will be the size of bricks. Long, wiggly bricks. There's Dad. He volunteered to host this tent."

Simon saw Mr. Mitchell instructing two other volunteers to stack fifty-four gummy blocks in eighteen alternating layers of three. The blocks rested on their long sides at a right angle to the three planks on the layer below.

"When it's your turn," Soraiya explained, "you remove one squiggly piece from any layer of the tower and place it on top. Play continues until someone pulls a block that causes the whole tower to come tumbling down."

"So," said Simon, "this is basically an exercise in structural engineering?"

"Exactly! By the way, did you know that 'kujenga' is a Swahili word meaning 'to build'?"

Simon shook his head.

"It's true. I did research. I always do research. You'll probably be great at this. You're good at figuring out puzzles and building stuff."

"Well, I don't know if—"

"I saw that thing you constructed in the library. The one Jack McClintock totally trashed with his pool noodle. It was amazing."

"Thanks, I guess. . . ."

"Hey, you should be proud. If that had been my Ferris wheel, I would've been proud."

The first four players started circling the jiggling tower. They took turns carefully extracting rubbery planks and then putting each piece on the top layer, making sure it was facing the opposite direction to the ones below.

It took about ten moves for the tower to come crashing down. The last player to make a move before the tower fell won.

"That's ten points for Carolyn Hudson!" shouted Mr. Mitchell. He officially noted and initialed the score on the card tucked into the plastic pouch behind Carolyn Hudson's number bib.

"Who's next?"

Soraiya shot up her hand.

"Okay, honey. Number one in my heart and on her bib, Soraiya Mitchell. Who else?"

Soraiya turned to Simon. "What're you waiting for? You miss all the shots you don't take."

"Okay, okay," said Simon, surrendering. He raised his hand.

"Number one-six-six, Simon Skrindle. Fantabulous. Step up to the tower. Who else?"

A bunch of hands shot up. Mr. Mitchell picked two. "Number thirty-seven, Odessa Pearce. And number one-oh-seven, Augusta Westhoff. You'll be our next four players."

Mr. Mitchell's assistants had already restacked the fifty-four blubbery bricks.

"Player with the lowest number goes first," said Mr. Mitchell. "That's you, Soraiya. Play will then continue clockwise around the tower."

That meant Simon would go fourth.

Soraiya delicately plucked a piece from the side of the tower and placed it on top. Odessa slid out a middle piece. Augusta went for one on the edge. In three turns, another three-piece layer was added to the top of the tower.

Simon studied the architecture of the tower and went for an edge piece he felt confident was not crucial to the tower's support. It felt like he was poking a jiggly cube of cold Jell-O in the fridge. He shoved the brick out with the palm of one hand, pulled it free with his other hand, then placed the slimy thing on top of the tower in the opposite direction to the layer that used to be the top.

Play continued for three more turns. Twelve more pieces were removed from their original positions. The tower was now five stories taller than it used to be. It was also looking less and less stable.

"Your turn, Simon," said Mr. Mitchell in the hushed tones of a TV golf announcer. Things were getting tense.

Simon tapped a gelatinous green block in the center of a layer.

And a bright-red LED inside the translucent slab started to throb.

Everyone in the tent who had ever played Kooky Kujenga gasped.

"Uh-oh," said Mr. Mitchell. "Simon, looks like you just picked the wobbler!"

To make his teetering-tower game even more exciting, Mr. Lemoncello had included one battery-powered brick that would quiver and quake the instant a player poked it.

"If you can successfully remove and place that plank," said Mr. Mitchell, "you will earn double points—if, of course, you go on to win the game!"

"Oooh," the crowd whispered in awe.

Simon did his best to steady his hand. He needed to carefully slide the shimmying brick out of the stack before it knocked out the two blocks along its sides.

He deftly extracted the wobbler with another delicate push and pluck.

The jiggly, blinking block was out of the tower.

Now all Simon had to do was gently, *very gently,* set the slab (which was wiggling like a real live gummy worm) on the tippy top of the tower, positioning it *just so* at the center of what would become the new highest level. A fraction of an inch off-center and the wobbler would shake the tower to its core and topple the swaying stack.

Simon took a deep breath.

Carefully, *very carefully,* he laid the shimmying brick down.

The tower did not collapse.

The audience oohed.

And Simon breathed a sigh of relief.

It was Soraiya's turn again.

"Well played, Simon," she said admiringly.

"Thanks."

Soraiya studied the tower.

"The wobbler jiggles elastically," she said aloud, even though it sounded like she was talking to herself. Then she mumbled a bunch of stuff about "angular velocity vectors" and "the precision of wobble" being different to "the line of nodes rotation."

Simon had no idea what she was talking about. He was more of a doer than a theorizer.

Finally, Soraiya slid a brick from somewhere close to the center. It came out pretty easily.

But she still had to place it on the tower's summit, alongside the wobbler.

It stayed put.

For two seconds.

Then it rumbled, slid sideways, skidded toward the edge, and knocked the whole tower off-kilter. All fifty-four rubbery, blubbery blocks tumbled to the ground, where they bounced and bobbled.

"Congratulations, Mr. Skrindle!" cried Mr. Mitchell. "You made the last successful move. You win with a wobbler!"

The crowd in the tent cheered.

"Way to go, Simon!" added Soraiya, who was probably the most non-sore loser Simon had ever met. "That move you made was amazing!"

"Let me see your scorecard, Mr. Skrindle," said Mr. Mitchell.

Simon gave him the cardboard sheet.

"Because you won with a wobbler," Mr. Mitchell explained, "you just earned *twenty* points—double what anyone can win in any of the game tents."

"Woo-hoo!" shouted Soraiya. "You're more than halfway home to the sidewalk board game, Simon, and that much closer to the titanium ticket!"

Hearing that shocked Simon a little. "Seriously?"

"Totally," said Soraiya. "You earned the points for winning *two* games by playing just one. That was very efficiently done. I love efficiency! Don't you? Where to next?"

"Huh?"

"We both get to play two more preliminary games, even though you really don't need to," said Soraiya.

She whipped a brochure out of her back pocket, scanned the Gameworks Factory Picnic app on her phone, and somehow still had a free hand to wave goodbye to her father. Soraiya Mitchell was very good at multitasking.

"Which one of these games would you be best at?" she asked. "We need to play to our strengths. For instance, I'm good at Mr. Lemoncello's Fantabulous Fourth Knight Free-for-All. There's another arena competition in the big blue tent in thirty minutes. The first one's already underway."

"Fourth Knight? I don't know that game. . . ."

Soraiya started speed-walking out of the tent. Simon followed her.

"Fourth Knight is huge online," Soraiya explained. "You and about a billion other players from all over the world are the fourth knight auditioning to join the king's elite three-member guard squad. You have to battle all the other players and some dragons and ogres to prove you're worthy. Last player standing wins."

They passed a booth that smelled like freshly made doughnuts, sugar, and cinnamon.

"I'm hungry," said Soraiya.

"Yeah," said Simon. "Me too. I sort of skipped breakfast."

Soraiya checked her watch. It was one of those that could tell her how many steps she'd taken and what her heart rate was. "Well, there's twenty-nine minutes before the next game starts. We should probably carbo-load like runners do before marathons. You want a fried butter ball? I think it's too early for a pickle pop."

"Um, I didn't bring any money," Simon said sheepishly.

Soraiya laughed. "You don't need money. This is a *Lemoncello* company picnic. Everything is free. Even the chocolate-covered bacon on a stick."

"That sounds good."

"Good?" said Soraiya. "It's delicious."

They went to the concession stand, picked up several red-and-white-striped paper trays filled with doughnuts, deep-fried Twinkies, and thick slices of chocolate-dipped bacon on wooden skewers, then found a spot at a picnic table.

"So," Simon asked, after gobbling down a doughnut stuffed with melted jelly beans and another one filled with lemon custard, "you're good at Fourth Knight?"

"I'm not good, Simon. I'm great. The way you were with Kooky Kujenga? That's me playing Fourth Knight."

"Then we should do that next."

"But you've never played before."

Simon nodded. "We don't have Wi-Fi at my house. My grandfather doesn't believe in it."

"He's the one who hates Mr. Lemoncello, right?"

"Yeah."

"That's too bad. I wonder if he hated him back when your mom and dad worked at the factory."

"My mother and father worked for Mr. Lemoncello?"

"Yeah. You didn't know that?"

Simon shook his head. "No. My grandparents never told me."

"Huh," said Soraiya. "I wonder why."

"Yeah," said Simon. "I wonder, too."

Jack McClintock limbered up his thumbs.

Once they were loose, he cracked his knuckles.

Then he linked his fingers and stretched them out.

"You warmed up?" asked his buddy Aiden.

Jack nodded. "This is the most crucial part of my battle plan, bro. The warm-up. The flex. Most wars are won before they're even begun. It's all in the prep and planning. And when the dust settles and this duel is done, I guarantee you: I will be the fourth knight chosen by the king. I *will* be in the sidewalk board game. I *will* take home the titanium ticket."

"I just hope I can come in second, man," said Aiden. "Then I'd be, like, the *fifth* knight!"

"Tell you what, bro. I'll slay you last. Take you out with a sponge dart."

"Thanks, man."

Jack and Aiden were in the blue video game tent. A giant twelve-foot-wide monitor was erected on an elevated platform at the far end. The screen was surrounded by rock-show-sized speakers. A loop of martial music blared as rotating images of knights of all shapes, sizes, and genders (all of them with bulging superhero muscles) danced in place like they were riding invisible bucking broncos in a rodeo. It was called the Hoss—its signature move, the Lasso—and was one of the many dance crazes inspired by Mr. Lemoncello's online video game. Another was the Boneless Chicken, where you had to flop around like a rag doll while clucking, "Bruck, bruck, bruck!"

Some of the computer-generated knights had cowboy hats or ski goggles or bunny ears or fluorescent-green hair. Some had all four. The costumes, including suits of armor made out of sparkly spandex, weren't exactly historically accurate.

Jack's avatar, the character he'd created and played with all the time, was up on the screen wearing camouflage armor and wraparound shades. He didn't wear a helmet, so everybody could check out his hair. It was slicker and blacker than an oil spill on a lump of polished coal.

The weapons weren't traditional Middle Ages stuff, either. Some knights carried lances and swords—but they were laser-guided lances and Wiffle swords with holes in the sides so they whistled when you swung them. Other knights were armed with rotten-egg bazookas or squeeze-bottle slime shooters. Some tried to start dart wars. One even had an automatic angry weasel launcher. Battles in Fourth Knight were always loud, funny, and messy, just the way Mr. Lemoncello liked them.

Jack saw two silhouettes enter the tent's brightly backlit entrance.

"You can talk to my dad about your parents later, Simon," said a chipper voice that Jack recognized from school. "Right now we need to focus on the games. Is there room for two more?"

"It's that brainiac Soraiya Mitchell," hissed Aiden. "From science. What's she doing here?"

"We'd like to sign up for the next Free-for-All," said Soraiya. (It was as if she'd heard Aiden ask his question.)

"You've got it, Miss Mitchell," said the adult signing up combatants and handing out the Lemoncello video game controllers. "How about you, Mr. Skrindle? Do you want to play?"

"Um, I guess so," Jack heard Skrindle say. "I've never played before."

"You'll need a controller," said the adult.

"What do these buttons do?" asked Skrindle, fiddling with the colored buttons and central joystick.

"Don't worry," Soraiya told him. "I'll give you a quick tutorial."

"What an I-D ten-T," sniggered Jack.

"Yeah," said Aiden. "That means 'idiot,' right?"

Jack ignored his friend. He was fully focused on crushing Simon Skrindle. The little weenie who had somehow bested the gate riddles outside Mr. Lemoncello's new supersecret building and figured out Ms. Pulliam's riddle. (Jack had followed him down the hall that day during lunch.)

They had to be flukes, Jack told himself. *No way is the village idiot better than me at anything!*

"All right," said the lady running the game, "we have our fifty players. I'm your referee, Mrs. Lauren Coffin from the boxing and shrink-wrap department. This will be a double-time Fourth Knight Free-for-All. You'll have fifteen minutes to find your weapons, build your barricades, dance your dances, wrestle the unicorn, toast marshmallows over a flaming dragon mouth, and, of course, storm the sandcastle before the king gives his toilet a royal flush and the walls wash away."

Jack laughed when he saw Simon staring at Soraiya after Mrs. Coffin ran through what would be a pretty basic fifteen minutes of game play. The poor guy had no idea of what kind of extreme chaos he was about to be plunged into.

"Hear ye, hear ye, knights and knaves," said Mrs. Coffin as the giant screen on the raised platform dissolved into an aerial view of a green medieval landscape that, strangely, also had skyscrapers and fast-food drive-throughs for knights on horseback (that's where you could pick up bonus life points if you ordered a salad instead of a cheeseburger). "Board the battle blimp. We are now flying over one of the castles of Mad King Ludwig. We drop in five, four, three, two, one! Good knight, it's time to fight!"

Jack jabbed his controller and leapt out of the blimp.

He knew how to aim his avatar just so to land on a warhorse that would carry him off to the pile of weapons in the town dump just over the first knoll faster than any other mode of transportation.

Except for the armored rhinoceros.

Which Soraiya Mitchell was riding.

She passed Jack on his right and grabbed a clump of low-flying Bongo Birds. Bongo Birds were worth fifty points and could be used as a screeching weapon.

Which Soraiya did! The angry birds screeched and wiped out ten contestants.

Simon Skrindle was one of the gamers eliminated by the Bongo screech. Soraiya thundered toward the Citadel of Sand on her charging rhino, doing a triumphant saddle dance.

Jack realized he'd made a tactical error.

He shouldn't have been focusing on Simon Skrindle. The goofus was only good at riddles and playing with blocks, not real games.

Surprisingly, it was the science nerd Soraiya Mitchell whom Jack needed to worry about.

Because, as he galloped across the Forbidden Island toward the sandcastle, all Jack could see in front of him was leathery rhino butt.

"This is stupendelicious!" cried Mr. Lemoncello as he marched through the exhibition halls of the secret building with Dr. Zinchenko and Mr. Raymo. "Hi-ho, Cherry-O, you two have done an amazible job back here!"

"Thank you, sir," said Dr. Zinchenko.

"Ditto," said Mr. Raymo.

Mr. Lemoncello swung open his arms to take in the vast expanse of the hall they were standing in. "This building, dear friends, will be my legacy! Not to be confused with my Legos at sea, which, hopefully, will float."

"But, if I may," said Dr. Zinchenko, "it is far too early for you to talk of your legacy. You're still young."

Mr. Lemoncello sighed. "True, true. But I'm not as young as I used to be. Why, I feel twenty-four hours older than I did yesterday. Oh, this looks like fun!"

Mr. Lemoncello scampered into a muggy atrium

featuring a giant submarine game, based on the Milton Bradley classic Battleship. Two fifty-foot-long and -wide wave pools, each one marked off into ten-by-ten grids, were separated by a tall wall, also blocked out in a 1–10, A–J grid. In the board game, players would alternate turns, calling shots at the other player's ships. In this larger-than-life version, they would ride in the open hatches of yellow submarines and toss water balloons over the dividing wall at each other—if they weren't swamped by a wave first.

"Do we have time to play a quick game?"

"Of course, sir," said Dr. Zinchenko. "The children are still in their preliminary, elimination games."

"You go on the other side, Chester, and set up your sub, and I don't mean a sandwich. I'll do the same on this side."

Mr. Lemoncello stepped off the edge of the pool and into one of the yellow submarine's two open hatches, right in front of the purple periscope. Wobbly battle balloons, filled with colored water, green sludge, and pink mayonnaise, were waiting for him in a cargo net down below.

The wave pool started undulating. Mr. Lemoncello shouted, "Cowabunga!" and piloted his mini-sub across the rolling surf toward a spot in the middle of the indoor ocean.

"Will this be one of the eight games the four lucky children get to play tonight?" he shouted to Dr. Zinchenko, who stood patiently at the side of the wave-swamped indoor pool.

"Yes, sir!" she shouted back. "Battleship is a classic. The victors of this game, and all the others, will be given a riddle, puzzle, or question that will move them closer to the ultimate goal—finding the titanium ticket."

"Excellent. Fire at will, Chester!"

A quivering water balloon flew over the dividing wall.

"A-eight!" shouted Mr. Raymo.

The balloon belly flopped in the D-4 square.

"Miss!" shouted Mr. Lemoncello. "This one is going . . . wherever it lands!"

He heaved up a water balloon.

"Oof," cried Mr. Raymo, his voice sounding slightly higher-pitched than usual. "Direct hit. I surrender. You win, sir."

"But I only fired one shot."

"It was a good one, sir."

Off in the distance, a grandfather clock started to sound its hourly melody.

"Oh, how I love the tintinnabulation of those bells, bells, bells," said Mr. Lemoncello, sailing his sub back to its docking slot. "Reminds me of our doorbell when I was a child!"

"Because, sir," said Mr. Raymo, emerging from the other side of the watery board game, "that is the classic doorbell melody, based on the Westminster chimes of the Big Ben clock tower in London."

"Those peals are so appealing," said Mr. Lemoncello. "Just like my banana shoes."

The clock chimed out twelve resounding bongs.

"It's noon," remarked Dr. Zinchenko, glancing at her

watch. "Only two hours until the Slippery-Sloppery Sidewalk Board Game on Main Street."

"Which means we are moving closer and closer to someone finding the first titanium ticket!" said Mr. Lemoncello. "Is it hidden in its proper position?"

"That it is, sir," said Mr. Raymo.

"Excellent!"

"Are you really certain you wish to go through with this, sir?" said Dr. Zinchenko. "The titanium ticket seems so dramatic. So, so . . . Willy Wonka–ish. So *Ready Player One*."

"As it should, Yanina. Are our Ohio friends in the air?"

"Yes, sir. The banana jet left Alexandriaville an hour ago. Kyle, Akimi, Andrew, and Haley are on their way."

"Wondermous. Now then, where is the dedication room? I'd like to see that before we return to the picnic festivities."

"First floor, sir."

When they reached the room, Mr. Lemoncello stepped up to one of its twenty-foot tall marble walls. Chiseled into the stone were these words:

THE FUTURE BELONGS TO THE PUZZLE SOLVERS.
THIS BUILDING IS DEDICATED
TO ALL THE CLEVER ENGINEERS
WHO HAVE MADE SO MANY
WILD AND FANTASTICAL IDEAS LEAP TO LIFE.
MOST ESPECIALLY SALLY AND STEPHEN SKRINDLE.

Mr. Lemoncello went over to the wall and rubbed his fingers along the notched names.

"Sally and Steve," he said softly. "If it weren't for them, there might not be a Gameworks Factory or even a Luigi L. Lemoncello. I owe them everything."

Mr. Raymo nodded. "True legends among us imagineers."

"I wish I had met them," said Dr. Zinchenko.

"Oh, you would've liked them, Yanina," said Mr. Lemoncello. "They weren't just incredibly clever. They were also kind, humble, and gracious. But as much as I miss them, I'm sure their son, Simon, misses them more."

Mr. Lemoncello sat down stiffly on a wide stone bench in the center of the room.

And for the first time that either Mr. Raymo or Dr. Zinchenko could remember, Mr. Lemoncello wept.

Simon thought Soraiya was amazing.

Eliminated from the Fourth Knight game, he stood gawking at the giant video screen. He and all the other players who'd been knocked out of the battle royal by Soraiya or Jack were now eager spectators. They watched Soraiya's and Jack's medieval-ish avatars (each carried gear that didn't exist back in the olden days) going up against each other in solo combat. One would be the last knight standing. Jack's character was swinging a war hammer with a squeaky plastic head that collapsed when it hit Soraiya's character's football helmet or hockey pads.

Each squeak lowered the life force of Soraiya's avatar.

"Yield!" shouted Jack.

"Never!" replied Soraiya, who, for the final round, had chosen a very peculiar weapon: a portable microwave oven, which she wore strapped to one arm like a boxy shield.

Jack swung his squeaky hammer. Soraiya popped open the microwave's door, snared the hammer's head, and slammed the oven door shut on it. Jack yanked hard on the handle but the hammer wouldn't budge. It was trapped inside the microwave.

With her free hand, Soraiya bopped a button on the appliance's control panel. "Time to bake the potato!" she shouted.

"Oooh," said a bunch of the vanquished players who knew more about Fourth Knight than Simon ever would. "She's baking the potato!"

"Pull her plug!" shouted one of Jack's buds.

"I can't!" Jack shouted back, sounding totally frustrated. "She upgraded to a battery-powered microwave!"

"Because I'm a smart shopper," taunted Soraiya.

"Oooh," said the crowd, enjoying the smackdown.

The microwave *DING*ed. The oven door popped open. Jack's sizzling war hammer was a shriveled lump of melted plastic.

It was also his final weapon.

While Jack's knight stood there, literally steaming, Soraiya's avatar leapt back into her rhino saddle and did a dance called the Uncle Wiggly. Finished, she dashed off to the sandcastle, where she quickly knocked King Ludwig off his throne (a golden toilet) just as he was about to give a royal flush.

"Not before you knight me!" Soraiya shouted.

"Very well!" cried the animated king, as nobly as he

could from his bathroom perch. "You, Soraiya Mitchell, are hereby declared the Fourth Knight!"

The crowd in the tent cheered.

Mrs. Coffin, the game supervisor, gave Soraiya ten points on her scorecard. Jack McClintock got five for second place. Simon received zero.

"You were fantastic, Soraiya!" Simon exclaimed.

"Thanks. I play every day after school. And Dad says I'm wasting my time. Ha! Okay, we each have one preliminary game left. I'm thinking about doing Math Mania. How about you?"

Simon tugged the crumpled games pamphlet out of his back pocket. He glanced at the one o'clock offerings. "Rock 'Em Sock 'Em Rebuses sounds fun," he said.

"Cool," said Soraiya. "I'll meet you afterward at the ice cream sandwich hut."

"Are those free, too?"

"Of course! Word of advice? Go for chocolate or vanilla. Stay away from ham and roast beef."

"Right," said Simon, urping a little at the thought of meat-flavored ice cream.

"Have fun!" Soraiya took off for her tent while Simon went looking for his.

And, of course, when he finally found the rebus tent, Jack McClintock was already inside.

"Get ready, gamers!" said the woman in charge of the rebus game from her perch on the stage.

A giant video screen behind her was filled with a Rock 'Em Sock 'Em Rebuses graphic, which spun in and out of a puzzle version of the same phrase with a rock, a sock, a pair of "M" candies, and a clump of buses labeled "Re."

"Fire up your devices, everybody, and go to Lemoncello-dot-i-t. This game will be played Kahoot!-style. If you don't have a phone, grab an lPad from one of my colleagues in the yellow vests."

Simon quickly learned that lPads were like iPads, but without the dot.

"Here you go, son," said the friendly guy holding a stack of them. "It's already open to the web page."

"Thanks."

"Choose a user name and enter game code one-seven-four-five," said the game host.

Thumbs tapped glass as all the players typed in their user names and the code.

The screen showed how many players were signing in. Twenty. Thirty. Sixty-three. Simon had chosen "Simon Says" for his screen name. He figured "Killer Jack" was Jack McClintock.

"Okay, gang," said the host through her head mic. "I'm getting a space alert. We've reached our maximum number of players. Sign-up is now officially closed. There will be a final game at one-thirty. We're going to do five rebuses, each with four possible answers. You have ten seconds to make your selection. Lemoncello-dot-i-t will instantaneously calculate your score and post a leader board listing the top ten players. You will earn points based on the speed and accuracy of your answer. You want to be fast but, more importantly, you *need* to be correct."

"This is your game, bro!" Aiden shouted at Jack.

"Hooah!" Jack shouted back.

They chest-bumped.

"Everybody set?" asked the game host, surveying the crowd. "Devices up! Here is your first puzzle."

One look, and Simon immediately knew the answer.

KNEE
LIGHTS

He waited for the four multiple-choice answers to fade into view and quickly tapped the third option, *neon lights,* because the puzzle showed the word "knee" on top of "lights."

The ten-second clock ticked down. The computer did its math. Simon waited. He glanced over at Jack McClintock, who was smirking, big-time. A bell *DING*ed. The answer was highlighted in Lemoncello yellow. Simon was correct.

Simon Says was on the leader board in third place.

Killer Jack was in first. Apparently, he'd been even quicker on the answer tap than Simon.

"Here's your second rebus!" announced the host.

D
UC
K

Simon chose the second answer, the one next to the triangle graphic: *sitting duck*.

The ten-second clock turned into a string of zeros. The computer calculated everybody's speed and accuracy.

Simon Says and Killer Jack were tied for second. Someone called Rebus Driver was in first, but not by much.

"We've hit the halfway point," said the host. "Here comes your third puzzle."

Simon focused on the screen.

M1Y L1I1F1E

Easy. Four ones inside the words "my life." He tapped the second choice, *For once in my life*.

Nine seconds later, he was in the lead!

Rebus Driver had dropped to ninth place. Killer Jack was in second.

"Two more," said the host. "It's still anybody's game. Remember, it's good to be fast, but it's better to be correct. Puzzle number four. Here we go."

The game was moving so swiftly, Simon didn't have time to swipe away the sweat trickling down his forehead.

A new puzzle appeared on the screen.

T_RN

It showed the word "turn" but without the letter "U."

Easy.

No U-turn was one of the answers. Simon selected it as quickly as he could.

The timer ticked down to zero.

No U-turn started to glow yellow. Simon had answered correctly.

He'd also ended up in first place! Killer Jack had dropped to third. Someone who went by the name Egg Head had squeezed into second.

"Wow," said the host. "What a tight race. Simon Says is in the lead, but the scores are so close, anybody could win with our final puzzle."

Simon felt someone staring at him.

He turned to look.

It was Jack McClintock. He was glaring at Simon.

Up came the final rebus.

DR. DR.

Simon, of course, immediately knew the answer. It had been a vocabulary word two weeks earlier at school. It meant "a statement or proposition that seems self-contradictory or absurd but in reality expresses a possible truth."

Like "Winning this rebus game could be the worst thing ever to happen to Simon Skrindle."

Because if Simon defeated Jack in front of the whole town, sure, he'd be a winner, but Jack would make his life miserable for years to come.

Plus, Simon might not need to win this rebus competition to move on to the sidewalk board game and then the secret building behind the factory. He'd earned all those bonus points playing Kooky Kujenga. He might still squeak into the next round.

He knew the answer was "pair of docs," or "paradox."

But should he play it?

He hesitated.

The countdown clock didn't. It kept ticking. It spun through its digits and locked down everybody's answer.

Except Simon's.

Because he had fretted so long, he didn't have time to tap one in. When the scores for the final question were tallied, Simon Says was no longer on the leader board.

He'd dropped out of the top ten.

Jack McClintock had won.

Simon met up with Soraiya at the ice cream sandwich stand.

"How'd you do?" she asked.

"Not so good."

"Who won? McClintock?"

"Yeah."

"But you're better at solving rebus puzzles than he is."

Simon shrugged, as if to say "whatever." But he knew Soraiya was right. He could've won. He *should've* won. He just needed to get out of his own way and do it.

"How was your Math Mash?" Simon asked, hoping to change the subject.

"Excellent," said Soraiya. "I came in first. Even aced the trick question where they asked what number you would get if you multiplied all the numbers on your cell phone's number pad."

"That sounds hard."

"Nah. It was easy. Because there's a zero. And zero times anything—or everything—gives you zero. I racked up another ten points, which, of course, pushes my total to twenty."

"I have twenty, too," said Simon. "From the Kooky Kujenga game."

"Where you were awesome."

"Or lucky."

"Luck had nothing to do with it, my friend," said Soraiya. "You just have mad skills."

That made Simon smile.

"You want an ice cream sandwich?" asked Soraiya, gesturing toward the menu board.

"They can really make ice cream that tastes like bacon, lettuce, and tomato?" Simon marveled.

"Yep. It looks like Neapolitan. Only it's pink, green, and red instead of chocolate, vanilla, and strawberry."

"Soraiya?"

"Yeah?"

"Can I show you something?"

"I guess."

Simon reached into his back pocket and showed her the engraved invitation from Mr. Lemoncello.

"Wow," said Soraiya. "Excellent calligraphy."

"Why does he want me to play these games so much?"

"Probably because you're the one kid in all of Hudson Hills who's never had the chance to enjoy any kind of Lemoncello fun."

"My grandfather says that years ago Mr. Lemoncello did something horrible to our family."

"Highly doubtful." Soraiya's watch started beeping. "We need to run. They're going to announce who's moving on to the Slippery-Sloppery Sidewalk Board Game in two minutes."

"Don't you want an ice cream sandwich?"

"We'll grab one later," said Soraiya. "To celebrate winning the next game! Let's go."

Simon and Soraiya hurried across the park and headed into the very crowded registration tent.

"Welcome back, gamers," said Dr. Zinchenko. The world-famous librarian was standing on a stage in front of a giant video monitor. "Our computers are currently finishing their tabulations. In just a moment, the names of the twelve contestants moving on will appear on this screen!"

"And that moment is now," said Mr. Lemoncello, appearing on the screen before any names did. "Computing the top scores was quite a complex task, much like doing the Chicken Cha-Cha-Cha at your cousin's wedding. Here, then, are the names of the twelve top scorers—all of whom are in for a messtacular afternoon!"

Trumpets sounded a fanfare. Drums rolled. Spotlights swung around the tent.

"Soraiya Mitchell!" boomed Mr. Lemoncello, as his image was replaced by swirling graphics spelling out names as he announced them. "Jack McClintock!"

"Booyah!" shouted Jack, somewhere to Simon's right.

Mr. Lemoncello kept going. "Shatar Shogi! Katie Grace! Carolyn Hudson! Skip Bo! Simon Skrindle!"

Yes! thought Simon. He even did an internal arm pump.

But on the outside he just looked shocked.

"Hey," said Soraiya, laughing, "do the math. If I made it with twenty points, then you had to make it, too!"

"Oh, right." Simon smiled. He was feeling pretty great.

Until he heard somebody over near Jack McClintock scream, "Simon Skrindle is the village idiot!"

"Oh, dear," said Mr. Lemoncello, reappearing on the screen. "Did I just hear an outburst of unsportsmanlike conduct from the young man in the backward baseball cap standing next to Jack McClintock? Blockhead move, Aiden. You were going to be our next contestant but, zertz! You are officially disqualified. Rude outbursts are against the sidewalk board game rules."

The rule book scrolled onto the screen.

One line was highlighted in neon green:

No rude outbursts permitted, Aiden.

"Now then, back to our contestants," said Mr. Lemoncello. "Zachary Koelsch! Quinn Connor! Ndeji Dibinga! Sofia Segura! And, last but not least, Piya Sarkarati!"

"Yes!" screamed Piya. "Yeeeeesssss! I'm in!"

Piya's enthusiasm made Simon, Soraiya, and just

about everybody else in the tent laugh. Even Mr. Lemoncello was laughing when he opened the center section of the TV screen as if it were a door in the middle of his face. He stepped through his own video image to join Dr. Zinchenko on the stage.

"Hearty and splendiferous congratulations to you, our twelve top-scoring contestants. You will now compete in this year's new and improved version of the sidewalk board game. Spoiler alert: It's going to be wet and wild. And, as you may have heard—unless you have waxy buildup in both of your ears, in which case, open a candle shop—the four winners of that game will be the first to see the marvels and wonders awaiting inside my amazamous new building behind the factory and have a chance to win a titanium ticket. But, I'm getting ahead of myself, which I sometimes do when I eat hard-boiled eggs before boiling water. Messy? Oh, yes. The yolk's on me. Dr. Zinchenko? Kindly explain how this year's sidewalk board game will be played."

"My pleasure, sir. This year, it's the Slippery-Sloppery Sidewalk Board Game. The object? Collect six flags."

"One of my favorite amusement parks, by the way," added Mr. Lemoncello.

"As in the past," said Dr. Zinchenko, "sections of sidewalk lining both sides of one block on Main Street have been painted to resemble board game squares."

"Thank you, Gameworks Factory Art Department!" Mr. Lemoncello said with a tip of his top hat.

A sly grin crossed Dr. Zinchenko's lips. "But, this year, we have added a few, shall we say, obstacles to the course."

"Of course we shall say that, Yanina, for that is what we have done!" said Mr. Lemoncello, waggling his bushy eyebrows. "You must land on all six red squares and complete the challenges awaiting inside their neighboring buildings. You have to pass the challenge to earn a flag."

"Each contestant will be assigned a different color," added Dr. Zinchenko. "Once you have collected six flags of your color, you must race up the middle of Main Street, through a Zoom Zone of rotating windmill blades, a bouncy house, the swinging rubber hammers of doom, and a chocolate volcano, to plant all of your flags in one of the florist foam islands floating in the center of our putrid putting green, which is only green because it is actually a pool of slime."

Simon gulped. And wondered what he'd just won his way into.

"Don't worry," whispered Soraiya. "It'll be fun."

Simon nodded and giggled nervously.

Dr. Zinchenko looked down at the contestants, who'd clustered at the lip of the stage. "The first four players to plant their six flags in the putrid putting green will be declared the winners and receive instructions about tonight's event inside the new building."

"Where," said Mr. Lemoncello, "you will have your chance to play another game and win the biggest, most stupendemous prize I've ever even thought about giving away. In fact, today's final game will be so intense, you'll need to partner with a world-class gamester to play it. Therefore, I have invited four of the sharpest gamers in all the land to join us today. They should arrive here in Hudson Hills . . ."

He glanced at his Mad Hatter–sized pocket watch.

"Right about . . . now!"

Simon heard the boom of a jet doing a flyby, the way they do before big football games. He and the eleven other contestants raced to the edge of the tent so they could watch the jet zoom across the sky and do a few air show stunts.

The plane was bright yellow.

It was also shaped like a banana!

"OMG!" said Soraiya. "That's Mr. Lemoncello's private plane. That's his banana jet!"

Mr. Lemoncello threw both of his arms up and addressed the crowd.

"Ladies and gentlemen, boys and girls, friends and families, on that jet heading for the nearest landing strip—and probably tossing their cookies because they weren't expecting a barrel roll *or* a loop the loop at such a low altitude—are four of my hometown heroes. You've seen them in my holiday commercials. You've watched them on the Kidzapalooza Network's *All-Star Breakout Game* show. You might even own their lunch box with the handy soup thermos. I know I do. Please welcome to the twenty-fifth annual Gameworks Company picnic the Lemoncello corporate jet carrying my fellow Buckeyes from Ohio—Kyle Keeley, Akimi Hughes, Andrew Peckleman, and, of course, the one, the only, Haley Daley!"

The crowd went wild.

"Each of the four sidewalk board game winners," explained Dr. Zinchenko, "will be teamed up with one of the Ohio players for tonight's high-stakes game inside the new building."

"I hope I get Kyle Keeley," whispered Soraiya. "That guy knows how to win."

"Yeah," said Simon, remembering the night he'd met Kyle and Akimi. "He's awesome."

Mr. Lemoncello put his hand to his ear, as if he were a news anchor receiving an update. "I've just been advised that the banana jet has landed safely. Mr. Mitchell? I believe you have an announcement to make."

Soraiya's dad made his way up a flight of steps to the stage. Mr. Lemoncello handed him a microphone.

"Thank you, Mr. L."

"You're welcome, Mr. M. But, please: No karaoke."

"No, sir. Just a quick announcement. We need our twelve players to head on over to the intersection of Main and Third Streets. Once there, put on your plastic jumpsuits, knee and elbow pads, and goggles. You'll also get to choose your helmets. Spectators? You should head over to Main and Third, too."

Mr. Lemoncello knocked knuckles with Mr. Mitchell, and then he and Dr. Zinchenko opened the door on the TV screen, stepped inside, and disappeared.

Simon couldn't help but slip around to the back of the stage to see where they'd gone.

But they weren't there. They'd really disappeared.

"How'd they do that?" he said to himself. "How'd they disappear?"

Soraiya walked up behind him. "I'd say magic, except as a scientist, I don't really believe in magic. Also, I can see the mirrors they used to achieve the illusion."

"Hurry along, you two," said Mr. Mitchell. "You don't want to be late to the starting gate!"

"What's up with the helmets?" Simon asked as he and Soraiya joined the throng making its way from the park to Main Street.

"You know how, when you play a board game, you pick a token?" said Soraiya. "The shoe, the boot, the robot. Well, since we're the playing pieces in the sidewalk board game, we have to wear safety helmets with big foam tokens on top. They're painted gold. They actually look pretty cool. Dad showed them to me last night."

There was a small U-Haul trailer parked at the corner of Third and Main. In the back were racks of waterproof coveralls (in various sizes) with elastic wrist and ankle cuffs, boxes of knee and elbow pads, and safety goggles dangling off a pegboard.

"We'll need all of that stuff and, of course, our tokens,"

said Soraiya. She grabbed a helmet with a lioness perched on top. Simon went with the penguin.

"You'll also need these," said the volunteer helping the contestants find the right-sized gear. She handed Simon and Soraiya high-tech watches. "They have your dice-rolling app. They're also waterproof."

Main Street was unrecognizable. The Zoom Zone, as Mr. Lemoncello called it, was set up in the middle of the road: a giant miniature-golf windmill with slowly moving blades; an inflatable bouncy house castle filled with a rainbow of colored balls and with a slide at its far end; an enormous double-headed rubber mallet, like something out of a cartoon, swinging back and forth over the street; a chocolate volcano burbling up slick syrup that slid down the slopes like sticky brown lava; and, at the far end of the street, a sludge puddle of oily slime with four islands of green florist foam floating near its center.

"That is so Lemoncello-y," said Soraiya, laughing as she checked out the final obstacle course. "We make it through that, we win! We see what's inside the new building before anybody else!"

"Um, okay," said Simon.

"It's like that classic show *Double Dare* on Nickelodeon!" said Piya as she surveyed the scene. "We're gonna get slimed!"

"Oooh, check out the sidewalks!" Soraiya said to Simon.

The first concrete square on the west side of the block

had the word "RUN" painted in big block letters on a pale-green background. There was also a red arrow pointing north. The rest of the painted sidewalk looked like a multicolored Monopoly or Family Frenzy game board.

"I guess that's the direction we need to go," said Simon, gesturing at the arrow.

"Well, duh!" said Jack, who'd snuck up behind Simon and Soraiya.

The token squatting on top of his helmet?

A snarling *Tyrannosaurus rex*.

The kind that ate anything and everything that got in its way.

"You know you don't belong here, right, Skrindle?" Jack sneered at Simon.

"Yes he does," said Soraiya.

"Ha!" said Jack, with a laugh. "We'll see about that."

The "RUN" square quickly became claustrophobic as all twelve players crammed into the four-by-four box.

"Jack?" said Piya, squeezing in beside him. "Two words. De-odorant."

"All right, gang," said a woman in a bright-yellow vest. Her ID tag read "Mrs. Leslie Zilber Blatt, Injection Molding." She pointed up the street. "There are ten squares on this side of the street. As you can see, some are painted red. Those are connected to shops where you'll go inside and complete your six challenges to earn your six flags. On this side, we've got the bakery, the ice cream shop, and the dentist's office. The purple squares in between are resting stops. Other painted pieces of sidewalk have stacks of cards you can pull. Lucky Duckies on the green squares are the good cards. The Clunkers on the blue squares? Well, those you want to avoid!"

"Unless you *are* a clunker," Jack muttered very close to Simon's ear.

"The crosswalks at both ends of the block are like the chutes in Chutes and Ladders," Mrs. Blatt continued. "When you step off the curb, you can slide across to the eastern side of the street. You'll find challenges at three more red squares—the cheese shop, the laundromat, and the pizza parlor. There are Lucky Ducky and Clunker squares over there, too. You will keep moving around the board until you complete all six challenges and have all six of your flags. Once you have all six flags, you need to run through the Zoom Zone, up the middle of Main Street."

"You still have time to quit, Skrindle," jeered Jack. "I'm sure that's what your grouchy old grandfather would want you to do anyhow."

For an instant, Simon wondered about that. Had Grandpa Sam figured out where Simon was? Because he definitely wouldn't like the idea of Simon being one of the twelve kids competing to be the first inside Mr. Lemoncello's secret new building, where he could, maybe, win a titanium ticket.

"Don't let Jack get under your dome," coached Soraiya. "At the Gameworks Factory, 'Fun is ingredient one.' My dad says that all the time. I think that used to be Mr. Lemoncello's advertising slogan."

"All right, contestants," said Mrs. Blatt, "kindly look at your watches. On the screen, you'll see a GIF of a waving flag. That's the color you need to collect."

Simon's flag was yellow. Soraiya's was green.

"Hooah!" cried Jack. "I am the black flag of death!"

Mrs. Blatt gave him a look. "Mr. McClintock?"

"Sorry. Just a little pumped."

"Try to contain yourself. Now then—everybody please note the randomly generated number on your flag. That is the order in which you will roll."

"Hooah!" Jack shouted again. His watch had just shown him he'd be going first. Soraiya drew the sixth position. Simon's flag had a twelve fluttering on it. He'd be going last.

"Ha!" said Jack, laughing. "Last is a good place for you to start, Skrindle. Because, guess what? That's definitely where you're going to finish!"

Simon stood on the "Run" square watching the other eleven contestants work their way up the western side of Main Street.

The dice-rolling app on their watches was only tumbling one die, which meant six was the maximum number of spaces anyone could move.

Jack had rolled a two, which put him on a Lucky Ducky square. He drew a green card the size of a poster board. The card told him he was due for his annual checkup so he could skip ahead six spaces and go to the dentist, one of the red squares with a challenge. He disappeared into the dentist's office and the other players rolled on.

Soraiya rolled a six, which took her to a red square on her first move. She scampered into the ice cream shop.

Simon hummed a soothing tune in his head until it was finally his turn. He threw a three.

That meant he was going into the bakery for his first challenge. As he was about to step through the door, he saw Jack come out of the dentist's office. He was covered with clear gunk that looked extremely sticky and gooey.

Jack wiped some of the stringy slobber off his goggles.

"Whoa! That big mouth in the chair can really rinse and spit!" he shouted. Then, very triumphantly, he held up a miniature black flag. It was dripping gobs of drool, too. "Hooah. Only five to go!"

Simon shuddered a little, then entered the bakery.

"Welcome, Simon," said the baker, Mr. Dylan Teut. "If I were you, I'd lower those goggles." Mr. Teut was dressed in a bulging baker's outfit that looked more like the padding police officers assigned to the K-9 squad used for training attack dogs. His goggles were already down. "Your first yellow flag is right there on the counter, stuck in a birthday cake."

"Thanks," said Simon. The floor was a checkerboard of black and white tiles. Simon took one step. His foot landed on a white tile.

Suddenly, a banana cream pie sitting on top of a display case flew up, catapulted by some kind of spring-loaded contraption. The pie slammed, whipped cream side first, into Simon's face.

That stunned him a little.

But he shook his head, wiped off his goggles, licked his fingers, and took another step forward.

This time, a whole pan of cupcakes leapt up, hurled

themselves across the room, and splattered him in a dozen different spots.

Simon cleaned frosting off his goggles, wiped some off his coveralls, and used his tongue to catch a chunk of cupcake that was sliding down his face.

"Mmm. That's good."

"Thank you," said Mr. Teut. "Life's better with sprinkles on top."

Simon looked down at his feet.

They were both on a white tile. So he picked up one foot and put it down, very carefully, on the nearest *black* tile and braced himself for impact.

Nothing new came flying his way. He took another step, making sure he stepped on a black tile again. No baked goods shot across the room. He had figured out how the game worked!

The future, and the flags, belong to the puzzle solvers, he thought. Yes, the game was messy. But Soraiya had been right. It was also fun.

Simon hopscotched his way to the counter, using nothing but black tiles all the way. He plucked the Fourth of July–sized yellow flag out of the layer cake, pausing to lick the frosting off its wooden stick. He was enjoying it so much, he forgot to pay attention to where he placed his feet when he turned around.

Two white tiles.

Two chocolate chip cookies came shooting out of the walls like ninja stars. Simon quickly clamped down on the flag with his teeth and caught the cookies as if they were flying Frisbees.

"Now that's what I call a balanced diet," joked Mr. Teut. "A cookie in each hand. Good luck on the rest of your quest, Simon."

"Thank you, sir!"

Simon hopped from one black tile to the next until he was safely out the door and back on the sidewalk.

Piya Sarkarati was standing on the red square, waiting to enter the bakery. Her eyes went wide when she saw the whipped cream and frosting smeared all over Simon.

Simon waved his flag. "I got my first one."

"Sweet," said Piya.

"Very. Want a cookie?"

"No thanks. Are those cupcakes smooshed on your chest?"

"Yeah. They're very delicious. You'll see!"

Piya laughed. "Thanks, Simon." She stepped into the bakery.

"Your roll, Mr. Skrindle," said Mrs. Blatt.

Simon tapped his watch. He couldn't believe his luck. He rolled another three that sent him to another red square! The ice cream shop. That's where Soraiya had started. He moved up the three spaces, wondering what wacky challenge might be waiting for him. He looked around, trying to find his friend—hoping she might give a hint about what to expect.

"Hey, Simon!" She was up at the corner, waving at him from the "Don't Walk" square.

He hadn't recognized her at first because her formerly white jumpsuit was now basically brown.

"Hot fudge!" she shouted, waving a green flag. "Enjoy your banana split!"

When Simon breathed out, he could see his breath. The whole ice cream shop was freezing.

Simon's next flag was poked into the top of a swirled mountain of whipped cream, right next to a bright-red cherry the size of a pumpkin. That whipped cream was on top of six huge scoops of ice cream (they were the size of exercise balls) smothered in gallons of gloppy hot fudge sauce. The whole ginormous sundae sat in a big blue wading pool of a bowl sealed inside a clear plastic cube.

"Th-th-there's only one w-w-way in to grab your flag," chittered a volunteer bundled up in a ski parka with a bushy fake fur collar. "You h-h-have to use the sl-sl-slide!" She (or he—it was hard to tell because they were so bundled up) pointed to a slide sculpted to look like a split banana.

And the slide was greased with gobs of mashed bananas.

"G-g-good luck!" said the volunteer. "And r-r-remember, in h-h-here, every d-d-day is Sundae!"

Simon scampered up the ladder to the slide, lowered his goggles, closed his eyes, and smeared his way down the slick chute of banana mush—headfirst and on his belly.

His sneakers were squishy when he came out of the ice cream parlor waving two flags—the hot fudge had melted some of the ice cream into a soupy puddle at the bottom of the baby-blue bowl. Some of it had soaked into Simon's socks.

Simon's next turn took him past the dentist's office challenge (he'd have to play this side of the street at least one more time) and onto the crosswalk. He scooted over to the other side of the street.

Where things got even grosser.

In the cheese shop, Simon had to crawl around in tunnels, burrowing through a holey wedge of Swiss cheese ten feet tall and twenty feet wide, searching for his flag. The holes were filled with stinky cheese sludge. But he finally found his flag.

"Gouda job!" said the lady running the cheese shop. "You're doing grate!"

"Thanks!" said Simon, laughing at the, yes, cheesy puns.

He made it to the laundromat on his next roll but had to wait on the sidewalk for a few minutes while the Gameworks volunteers inside "reset the props."

Apparently, a lot of the props were soap-related.

Because when it was Simon's turn to go in and face his challenge, he had to trudge across an indoor lake of soapsuds fizzing up to the ceiling while he dodged clear plastic "bubble" balls.

Simon hoped he wouldn't slip as he sloshed across the floor like a human mop, his squeaky sneakers scrubbing up foamy bubbles.

To release his flag, Simon climbed into a human-sized hamster wheel called "the spin cycle." In his head, he heard a heroic musical anthem. It pumped him up. He churned his legs and spun the wheel faster and faster. As he did, sudsy water rose up inside a tube and triggered a lever that knocked a rubber ducky off its perch. The squeeze toy ducky was proudly carrying a tiny yellow flag poked into its air hole.

"Yes!" Simon shouted as he plucked it out.

Simon emerged from the laundromat soaked but carrying four flags.

"Way to go, Simon!" hollered Soraiya from across the street. She was waving four flags, too.

Jack had *five*. But the dice weren't rolling his way.

"Aw, come on, you dumb watch! I needed a two, not a three!"

It sounded like he'd just missed the one red square he still needed and would have to take another lap around the board.

Back on the west side of Main Street, the dice app

on Simon's wrist made a *WHOMP-WHOMP-WHOMP* noise and sent him to a Clunker card.

"You're overdue for your annual appointment," it said. "Go see the dentist. Immediately!"

Huh. Simon was confused. A Lucky Ducky card, one of the good ones that gave players a bonus, had sent Jack to the dentist. Why was a bad card, a Clunker, sending him to the same red square challenge?

He found out soon enough.

His yellow flag was planted in the braces bracket of a wide-open plastic model of a mouth. It was larger than an enormous car's trunk. Thick drool was dribbling out of the cartoonish mouth—explaining why Jack had come out soaked in slobber. Extracting the flag would be nasty enough. But getting to the mouth would be the hard part.

"Oooh, you must've pulled a Clunker," said Dr. Gregg Lituchy, the town's dentist, who had turned his office into a sidewalk board game stop. "Because, Simon, it looks like you have a few cavities that need drilling!"

He pressed his foot on a pedal. A high-pitched whine sent shivers down Simon's spine.

Then things got even worse.

Two dozen Nerf drill bits spun their way down from the ceiling. Others poked up from the floor. Some flung toothpaste off them with every spin. To get to the slobbering open mouth to yank out his flag, Simon would first have to dance his way through a maze of whirring drill bits, all trying to block his path or knock him on his butt.

And there were dental floss trip wires stretched across the floor, too.

It took some time, but Simon was able to figure out a route through the maze and extract the flag from the slobber mouth with a pair of pliers Dr. Lituchy lent him.

"Good work, Simon," said Dr. Lituchy. "Nobody else figured out the maze that quickly."

With five flags in hand, Simon needed only one more—from the Pizza Palace on the east side of the street. He made it to the red square outside the Italian eatery on his next orbit around the outdoor board game.

He stepped inside and the air smelled delicious. Like he'd just stuck his head inside a steaming pizza box.

"Buongiorno," said the owner, Mr. Myles Decosimo. "Your flag is hidden inside a plastic meatball, which is hidden inside that giant bowl of spaghetti and meatballs."

So Simon had to climb into a clear glass bowl that was larger than a hot tub and feel his way around the warm, squishy noodles swimming in tomato sauce. After diving into the muck several times and getting oregano up his nose, he found a plastic meatball he could pry open like a toy Easter egg.

His sixth and final flag popped out.

Simon climbed out of the bowl, with strands of spaghetti dangling off his nose, coveralls, and shoes. Back on the sidewalk, he wiped the red sauce off his watch and tapped his next dice roll. It took him to the southeast corner of the block—the launching pad for his sprint through the final obstacle course in the center of Main Street.

"You need to wait there, Simon," said Mrs. Blatt. "There's congestion in the Zoom Zone. Three players at a time is the limit."

So Simon remained on the "Free Standing" space and waited.

"Hello, Loser McSnoozer," whispered someone behind him.

Simon turned around.

Jack McClintock was covered in soapsuds but had six black flags tightly gripped in his fist.

"Looks like we'll be zooming through the Zone together," he whispered so no one else could hear. "If I were you, I'd start saying my prayers."

With Jack more or less breathing down his neck as they both waited on the "Free Standing" square, Simon watched the three contestants working their way through the Zoom Zone in the middle of Main Street.

Piya had already made it to the putrid putting green and sloshed her way through the knee-deep slime to plant her six flags in one of the bobbing cubes of foam.

"That's my daughter!" screamed her mother in the crowd. "The future is female! Woo-hoo!"

Piya would be the first contestant moving on to the supersecret building.

Soraiya had already made it through the giant windmill—a monster-sized version of the Putt-Putt classic—and the bouncy house. Now she was timing her pass under the swinging, double-headed rubber mallet. It was suspended from the apex of a steel triangle. Both sides of the rubber mallet were ridged, like a kid's squeaky toy. When the path was clear, Soraiya turned sideways and dashed through the hammer obstacle. It barely missed her, whooshing past as it made another pendulum swing.

"Yes!" shouted Simon.

"She got lucky," huffed Jack beside him.

Next, Soraiya had to scale the slopes of the chocolate volcano.

As she climbed up, Carolyn Hudson slipped and surfed back down to where she'd started, riding a wave of fudge sludge.

"Grab the handholds!" Soraiya yelled over her shoulder from her perch at the crater where lawn sprinkler jets of chocolate sauce sprayed up into the air. "They're hidden under the chocolate. It's just like climbing a rock wall!"

"Thanks!" shouted Carolyn, who'd already started working her way back up the volcano.

"What a fool," snorted Jack. "You never give aid or comfort to your enemies."

Soraiya and Carolyn both conquered the mountain, slogged across the green swamp of the putrid putting green, and planted their flags.

The crowd cheered. The first three contestants moving on to the titanium ticket round—Piya, Soraiya, and Carolyn—joined (somewhat slimy) hands and raised them triumphantly.

"All right, boys," said Mrs. Blatt. "You two are up

next. We have three winners. We only need one more! On your marks, get set, lemon, cello, go!"

Simon tightened his grip on his flags and took off. Unfortunately, Jack *blasted* off. He paused at the windmill, waited for the blades to clear, and dashed through.

Simon matched Jack's moves and cleared the windmill, too, although he did feel a blade brush against his back.

Now they were both in the bouncy castle, where the floor was basically a ball pit. Jack was attempting to plow his way through the sea of plastic balls. Simon took a more nimble, high-stepping approach and made it to the exit ahead of Jack. He jumped up and scooted down the slide at the far end. When he landed, he was face to face with the swinging rubber hammers of doom.

"Go ahead, Skrindle," cried Jack, who'd just slid down from the bouncy house. "You made it here first. You can have first dibs on the hammer swing."

Whoa, thought Simon. *That's a surprise. Jack's being a good sport.*

"Um, thanks, Jack."

Simon crouched down and studied the hammer as it moved back and forth. He could smell the rich milk chocolate flowing down from the volcano obstacle on the other side. He timed his takeoff perfectly and dashed to where the hammer head had just cleared.

"Whoa!" shouted Jack. "Is that your grandfather?"

Simon paused. Whirled around.

"W-w-where?"

"Never mind," said Jack. "It's just some other old geezer."

And that's when the rubber hammer swung back and conked Simon in the head. He toppled to the asphalt, which, fortunately, was covered with foam matting.

"Don't say I didn't warn you, Skrindle!" shouted Jack as he cleared the hammer and scurried toward the volcano. "No aid. No comfort. Hooah!"

Feeling a little dizzy, Simon hauled himself up off the ground.

The hammer knocked him down again on its return swing.

Dizzy, Simon tucked and rolled. He didn't want a third hammer whack.

Stumbling to his feet, he staggered toward the slippery chocolate slope. Thanks to Soraiya, he knew to look for handholds. But he could only use one hand; the other one was busy clutching his six flags. His vision was also a little blurry.

He slogged his way up the slope. Jack must've slipped and slid a little on his climb, because he and Simon made it to the summit of the chocolate volcano at the exact same second. Chocolate sauce was spewing up from the crater, showering them both with muddy brown liquid.

"How's your head?" jeered Jack, under his breath.

Kind of woozy, thought Simon. He didn't have a concussion (the rubber hammer was just a giant squeak toy), but he did feel wobbly.

"So long, Skrindle!" shouted Jack.

Simon heard his opponent jump, land on his butt, and sled down the far slope. So he tried to mirror Jack's moves.

But his goggles were smudged with fudge, so he was sort of flying blind.

Groggy, he jumped up like he'd heard Jack do.

But Simon didn't hit the slope.

KERPLUNK!

He plopped, butt first, into the three-foot-deep crater. The powerful chocolate jets knocked all six flags out of his hand.

"Noooo!" Simon cried as the flags he'd worked so hard to collect were washed away in the surge. Completely drenched in chocolate, Simon used both hands to grab hold of the rim of the crater and haul himself up. He must've looked like a chocolate groundhog, popping up from its hole.

Because as he watched his flags slosh down the sides of the mountain, everybody on Main Street was pointing up and laughing at him.

Hysterically.

Except Jack McClintock.

He was too busy planting his six flags in the putting green and becoming the fourth and final contestant moving on to the next round.

Defeated, Simon slid down the side of the chocolate mountain.

A volunteer guided him to the outdoor shower tent, where he was able to hose off all the goop and glop he'd been slimed with during his failed attempt to win the game. He then passed under a car-wash-sized hot-air blower to dry his hair and face in a flash.

His own clothes had remained clean under the high-tech waterproof coveralls.

"Would you like a souvenir T-shirt?" asked a volunteer.

"No thanks," he mumbled.

He slumped his shoulders and shuffled out of the tent.

"Simon?" Soraiya called to him. "Are you okay?"

"Yeah," Simon told her. "But you know that thing you say about the future belonging to the puzzle solvers?

You're wrong. The future belongs to cheaters like Jack McClintock. Always has, always will."

"What'd Jack do?"

"Nothing."

"You want to register a complaint with Mrs. Blatt?"

"No, Soraiya. I want to go home."

He worked his way through the wall of spectators lining Fourth Street and sidled through the mob behind them on the next block of Main Street.

It felt like everybody in Hudson Hills was laughing at him.

Probably because they were.

Everybody except Soraiya. She was looking at Simon with pity in her eyes. That was almost worse than all the pointing and laughing.

As he walked up Main Street, moving farther and farther from the festivities, Simon could still hear the loudspeakers making announcements back at the sidewalk board game.

"Well, folks, there you have it," a booming voice (it sounded like Mr. Mitchell) declared. "We have our four winners! They will be the first to see what's inside the supersecret new building behind the factory. That'll happen today at six p.m. when they will play an exciting new game to win a titanium ticket, which could be their ticket to an out-of-this-world, unbelievable, and yet-to-be-announced prize!"

Simon glanced at his watch (they'd let him keep it).

There were still three hours before the game in the super-secret new building.

The one Simon wouldn't be playing.

"All right," Mr. Mitchell's amplified voice continued. "Here are the teams going on to today's final game."

Simon sat down on a park bench to listen. The block between Eighth and Ninth Streets was pretty much deserted. There was no one there to laugh at him.

"First up," Mr. Mitchell's voice echoed in the distance, "Carolyn Hudson! You'll be playing with the star of Kidzapalooza's *Hey, Hey, Haley,* the one, the only, the Grammy Award–winning Haley Daley!"

The crowd roared. From four blocks north, it sounded like a dragon waking up from a long winter nap.

"Jack McClintock?" Mr. Mitchell continued. "You'll be heading into the next game with Andrew Peckleman. Piya Sarkarati? You'll be playing alongside Akimi Hughes. And, Soraiya Mitchell? Don't worry, we didn't forget you. Your partner will be the legendary gamester himself, Kyle Keeley!"

There was another excited roar from the crowd at the outdoor board game.

Simon was happy for Soraiya. She deserved to team up with Kyle Keeley, the top gamer from Ohio.

Simon wasn't sure what he would do next. Go home and build something? Maybe play with his glockenspiel? Or, he could go eat one of those BLT ice cream sandwiches. . . .

Suddenly, a yellow minibus, shaped like a lemon on wheels, whirred up the street. It stopped in front of Simon's bench. The door swooshed open. There was no one sitting in the driver's seat. Akimi Hughes, however, was buckled into the first swivel chair behind it.

"It's an autonomous automobile," she said when she saw the look on Simon's face. "That means it drives itself."

"Um, why's it shaped like a lemon?"

"What? You think Mr. *Lemon*cello would make his driverless minibus look like some other kind of fruit? Hop in. This is your ticket to ride."

"Where are we going?"

"You're Simon Skrindle, right?"

Simon nodded.

"You're the one Kyle and I met like a week ago. The one who nailed all those riddles."

"I was just—"

"We need your help."

"You do?"

"Yes. I just said so."

"Oh. Right."

"Kyle Keeley's sick. Dr. Zinchenko thinks it's a stomach virus. Some kind of twenty-four-hour bug. Then again, she's a librarian. Not a medical doctor . . ."

"But Kyle's supposed to play the final game with my friend Soraiya."

"Exactly. So, we need a substitute. Guess who?"

"Um, Miguel Fernandez? Sierra Russell?"

"Nope. They're both back home in Ohio. We need you."

"To do what?"

"To take Kyle's place."

The self-driving lemonmobile whisked Simon and Akimi up the steep roads leading to where the Gameworks Factory sat perched on the bluff overlooking the Hudson River.

"We're going to the factory?" Simon asked.

"Uh, yeah," said Akimi, nodding toward the tablet computer operating the autonomous vehicle. "See?"

There was a box labeled "Destination" with "Loading Docks/Mr. Lemoncello's Gameworks Factory" typed on it. Simon thought it was weird to see the oval minibus steering itself and doing exactly what the street signs and traffic lights told it to do.

"This is just a bigger version of Mr. Lemoncello's Looney Lemons and Limes Robo-rally Race Car game," said Akimi.

"I've never heard of it."

"Seriously? It's been a big hit for years."

"I'm not allowed to play Lemoncello games."

"Why not?"

"Long story."

"Well, you're about to play the biggest, most important Lemoncello game ever created. It's Mr. Lemoncello's masterpiece." Then Akimi gestured for Simon to lean in so she could whisper something to him. "It's what we were testing that night we met!"

"Was it fun?"

"Fun? Hello! It's a Lemoncello! It's also a mind bender. You need to be a genius to figure out the whole thing. Kyle and I never did. We ran out of time. And, from what Dr. Zinchenko and Mr. Raymo tell us, they've upped the degree of difficulty even more with all new games and riddles." She shrugged. "Guess they had to because the prize is totally out of this world."

"What is it?"

Akimi shrugged again. "Nobody knows. But we will. Probably right around six o'clock."

The electric lemonmobile whirred itself around to the back of the Gameworks Factory and the loading docks, where dozens of eighteen-wheeler trucks were parked, ready to take Monday morning's shipments of Lemoncello games all across the country.

"We're in the red one," said Akimi.

Simon nodded. "Okay. How come?"

"We needed a place to hang out between the time we landed and the big game. They built us a couple of dressing rooms and a little lounge inside the trailer. We were able to watch the sidewalk board game on a video monitor."

"Oh. I didn't do so well."

"Uh, yeah. Because, from what we saw, it looked like that guy in the T. rex helmet distracted you—right before the swinging hammer of doom bonked you in the head. By the way, how's it feeling?"

"Fine, now. It just made me a little wobbly when I reached the top of the volcano."

"Yeah," said Akimi. "We saw."

Hydraulics whooshed as the lemonmobile came to a stop alongside the red truck.

"You have arrived at your destination," said a computerized voice from the dashboard.

The door swung open.

"Come on," said Akimi, stepping out of the vehicle. "You need to work with Haley Daley."

"How come?"

"She has a whole trunk of costumes and wigs. She brought all her Hollywood makeup stuff, too. You need to become someone other than Simon Skrindle."

"Huh?"

"Simon Skrindle didn't win a slot in tonight's big game. So, guess what? You're going to become somebody else!"

"Isn't that cheating?"

"No. Because you can't win. Just like I can't win. And Andrew and Haley can't win. We can only help the kids from Hudson Hills win."

"But I'm from Hudson Hills."

"Simon?"

"Yes?"

"You're not going to be you. You're going to become someone new. We need you to do this. Soraiya needs you to do this."

Simon thought about what Akimi was telling him. "I can't win?"

"That's right. Unless, you know, Mr. Lemoncello decides to bend the rules."

"So if I can't win, I'm not cheating. I'm just putting on a disguise to help Soraiya?"

"Exactly. It's what Mr. Lemoncello would want you to do."

"Seriously?"

"Yep. He's all about helping people."

"But, do you really think I can fool people into thinking I'm someone I'm not?"

"Absolutely. Haley is amazing. She's learned so much in Hollywood and can do all sorts of cool tricks with plastic, glue, and foam. You can be anyone you want. For instance, I'm not really Akimi Hughes. I'm Miguel Fernandez!"

She grabbed her left cheek with her right hand and started to tug like she was going to pull off her face.

"You're kidding!" said Simon, a little freaked out.

"Yes," said Akimi, letting go of her face. "I am."

Simon laughed. "Okay. Let's do it."

"Great."

He followed Akimi up a short flight of concrete steps to the loading dock and went over to the roll-up door on the back of the long red rig.

Akimi pushed a button. A regular-sized door, hidden inside the roll-up door, popped open. Kyle Keeley was standing on the other side.

He had a blanket draped over his shoulders and an ice pack sitting on top of his head like a floppy hat. He was also carrying a steaming mug of chicken soup.

"Simon's in!" Akimi announced.

"Yes," said Simon, and this time he didn't hesitate. "I am."

"Okay," said Haley, studying Simon's face. "We can work with it."

She opened up a large fishing tackle box filled with makeup supplies.

"Brainstorm! I'm going to give you a prosthetic nose made out of latex."

"Okay," said Simon. "What do you want me to do with it?"

Haley laughed. "Wear it, silly. Don't worry. In Hollywood, we're masters of disguise. I learned how to make noses and chins and fake body parts from the makeup artist who did *Zombie Dance Party 3000* for Kidzapalooza. I was one of the zombies. The blond one. We should give you a different chin, too. And a wig. A shaggy mop top. And cooler glasses."

"How about his costume?" asked Akimi.

"I'm thinking a white T-shirt and a black leather jacket on top of jeans and new kicks!" said Haley. "Total 'cool dude' look."

"I'm, uh, really not all that cool," mumbled Simon.

"Work with me, Simon!" said Haley. "Sometimes you just have to fake it until you make it!"

"Um, okay."

Simon tried to remember how Jack acted. Gave himself a little swagger. A little bluster.

"Yeah," he said in a strong, confident voice. "I can be this guy."

"Woo-hoo!" said Akimi.

"Take a seat, Simon!" said Haley. "It's showtime!"

One hour later, Simon didn't recognize the kid looking back at him from the mirror.

Instead of his fuzzy buzz cut, he had shaggy black hair that fell down to his eyes. He also had a pretty big nose, bushy black eyebrows, a chin with a dimple in the middle, and thick-rimmed glasses.

"Remember," Haley coached him, "acting is believing. If you believe you are someone different, you will become someone different."

"Yeah," said Simon. "Cool."

"Walk like this," coached Haley. "Hold your head up. Chest out. Shoulders back. There you go. You've got it!"

Andrew Peckleman came into the dressing room. "Who's this guy?" he whined, shoving his goggle-sized glasses up the bridge of his nose with a finger. "I thought we decided that kid Simon was going to play with Soraiya."

"It is Simon," said Akimi.

"No it's not," said Andrew. "Simon has short hair."

"It's a wig," said Akimi. "Good job, Haley."

"I know," she said.

"And we can't call him Simon anymore," said Akimi. "He's, uh, Mario!"

"Mario?" said Simon.

"Yep," said Akimi. "Because you kind of look like that guy from the video game. You know, Super Mario. But without the hat or mustache."

"Yeah," said Simon, turning up the confidence. "I shaved this morning." He tried snapping his fingers and humming a tune a cool dude might hum.

"Awesome!" Kyle Keeley, sounding much better than he had earlier, squeezed into the makeshift dressing room. "You look amazing, Simon. I didn't even recognize you."

"Kyle?" said Akimi, arching an eyebrow.

"Yeah?"

"Shouldn't you be lying down?"

"Huh?"

"You're sick, remember?"

"Oh, right." Kyle put his fist over his mouth and looked

like he might hurl. “Just wanted to make sure Simon was all set.”

“I am good to go, bro,” said Simon.

“Awesome!” said Haley. “Now, let’s just hope Soraiya Mitchell doesn’t recognize you, either!”

"Welcome, ladies and gentlemen, boys and girls, squirrels and chipmunks!"

Mr. Lemoncello stood on a raised platform decorated with scalloped yellow bunting that resembled sugar-sprinkled candy lemon slices. He was addressing the crowd that had migrated uphill from the sidewalk board game to gather in front of the new mirrored building. The shimmering silver walls reflected the crimson sky as it made its way toward twilight.

Heavy lemon-yellow drapes covered what appeared to be a sign on the arched, four-story-tall roof over the building's main entrance. All the security gates and fencing had been removed overnight. The security puppies had found loving forever homes at the picnic's pet adoption booth. Now there were a pair of sweeping fieldstone paths winding their way through a lush lawn, past topiaries and a koi pond (filled with fish and plastic windup scuba divers), to the towering front doors.

Dr. Zinchenko and Mr. Raymo stood on the small stage with Mr. Lemoncello. Dr. Zinchenko was applying a new coat of bright-red lipstick, using the disco ball building behind her as a gigantic makeup mirror.

"First of all," said Mr. Lemoncello, addressing the crowd, "I would like to personally congratulate the four winners of the sidewalk board game. Congratulations, congratulations, congratulations, congratulations. Now then, winners, as you've heard, you will be playing another awesometastic game—starting in about thirty minutes. Your chance to win a titanium ticket! Actually, to call it a game is a little misleading. It's the first of a series of games—to be played here and elsewhere. A March Madness tournament leading to the biggest, most stupendous prize I have ever given away. One worth millions and billions and bazillions of dollars!"

The crowd oohed, aahed, and whistled.

"Today, I am pleased as punch—the fruity stuff with ginger ale and sherbet, not the ones to the nose or belly—to announce the true purpose of this new building. My dear friends, in appreciation for all that you do here at Lemoncello Gameworks, henceforth, fence forth, and forever more, Hudson Hills, New York, won't just be the home to the factory that produces my marvelously wonderful games. It will also be the home of my masterpiece, one of the new wonders of the modern world, and I'm not talking about a loaf of bread. Oh no. This is the brand-new, spectacularrific, highly interactive, soon-to-be-world-famous Board Game Hall of Fame!"

Mr. Lemoncello slapped a big green button.

Rippled fabric wafted away from the top of the main entrance to reveal a spectacular sign etched into the glistening glass.

WELCOME TO THE
BOARD GAME
HALL OF FAME

A thousand biodegradable balloons stuffed with birdseed were set free. T-shirt cannons pummeled the crowd with the hall of fame's first souvenirs. Fireworks sizzled and spewed from mortars hidden on the building's roof.

"The Board Game Hall of Fame is basically an indoor amusement park with some of the most amazing exhibits ever created by the wizards on my imagineering team!"

"Why, thank you, sir," said Mr. Raymo, blushing.

"Inside these glass walls," Mr. Lemoncello continued, "all your favorite board games will come to bigger-than-life life. Why, there's a Rubik's Cube the size of a small house. You can zoom around a room on flying dragons that just escaped from a dungeon. You can even play Rush Hour in an indoor parking lot where you'll drive battery-powered cars, semitrailers, and a boxy ice cream truck!"

The audience applauded.

"We won't be showing you folks out here what the kids will encounter inside the museum tonight. Because we don't want to ruin any of the surprises when it's your turn to explore the Board Game Hall of Fame. However, a local jug band will be dropping by to entertain us for the next two hours. I, myself, will juggle. Dr. Zinchenko brought her kazoo, and everything in the snack tents is, of course, free!"

"T-minus twenty minutes and counting, sir," Mr. Raymo whispered to Mr. Lemoncello.

"Oh, boy!" Mr. Lemoncello flapped his hands together, giddy-seal-style. "Our inaugural Board Game Hall of Fame game will commence in twenty minutes. Tonight's competition will be intense. It might even be unbridled and ferocious, especially if someone brings a horse or a tiger. As you've heard, to help our four local winners navigate the ins and outs of the multilayered game play, we've flown in four of the greatest gamers in all the land."

The high school marching band did a drumroll. Searchlights swung across the stage. A hush fell over the crowd.

"From Alexandriaville, Ohio," boomed Mr. Lemoncello, "please welcome Andrew Peckleman! Akimi Hughes! Haley Daley! And Kyle Keeley!"

The crowd cheered as three of the Ohio gamers bounded onto the stage and waved to their many fans.

"Oh, dear," said Mr. Lemoncello, doing a double take. "Where's Kyle?"

Dr. Zinchenko whispered in his ear.

"Is that so?" said Mr. Lemoncello. "Is he forcing fluids, sucking peppermints, and staying close to a commodious commode?"

Dr. Zinchenko nodded.

"Good!" said Mr. Lemoncello. He turned back to the crowd. "Ladies and gentlemen, boys and girls, turtles and doves. I regret to inform you that this afternoon, while watching the sidewalk board game, Kyle Keeley grew violently ill. Therefore, he will not be able to participate in this evening's activities. However, we are very fortunate that, at the very last minute, we were able to locate one of the greatest gamers I have ever met to take his place. A true genius if ever I saw one. The kids from Ohio call him Mario, so you can, too! Please, put your hands together for the one, the only Mario!"

Head up, shaggy black wig bobbing, Simon and his big fake nose strode onstage. He raised up both arms like he'd seen a boxer do once on TV.

"Marr-ee-oh!" the crowd chanted. "Marr-ee-oh!"

Simon smiled.

So far, pretending to be someone he wasn't was totally awesome.

Simon, disguised as supergamer Mario, followed the Ohio kids as they walked along the line of Hudson Hills winners and, like sports teams do at the end of a game, shook everybody's hand.

"Congratulations," he said to Carolyn Hudson (they had math together).

"Thank you, Mario!" she gushed. "I think you're even cuter than Kyle Keeley."

Simon did what he figured a cool dude would do. He winked at her. "Thanks."

He shook hands with Piya Sarkarati (she lived right across the street from his grandparents!). Piya didn't recognize him. For once, being a practically invisible kid at middle school was really paying off.

"Hey, Mario," said Jack McClintock, grabbing Simon's hand with both of his and pumping his arm. "Good to

have you in the game, dude. Although, to be honest, I was really looking forward to going one-on-one against the legendary Kyle Keeley. I was going to *own* him, big-time."

"Aha," was all Simon could manage in reply.

Finally, he shook hands with his partner, Soraiya.

"This is so cool!" she said. "Mr. Lemoncello says you're one of the best gamers he's ever met! We are so going to win this thing!"

"Booyah!" said Simon, because he'd heard some guys at school say it when they were pumped.

"All right, everybody," said Dr. Zinchenko. "If you haven't done so already, please find your partner."

"You're with me," Andrew Peckleman said to Jack McClintock.

"Who are you again?" said Jack.

"Andrew Peckleman. Kicked out of the Escape game, redeemed in the Library Olympics, made a minor splash in *Mr. Lemoncello's All-Star Breakout Game*?"

"Oh, right. You're the guy Charles Chiltington pushed around."

"Ancient history!" said Andrew, his face turning pink. "Ancient history!"

"Don't worry," said Jack with a sinister grin. "You're my perfect partner."

To their right, Carolyn Hudson was jumping up and down, saying, "Omigosh, omigosh, omigosh. You're you! I can't believe it. You're really Haley Daley. You smell like chocolate chip cookie dough!"

Haley fluffed out her golden hair. "You like the cookie dough scent? It's the newest in my line of Haley Daley Daily Shampoos. Also available in kiwi-lime and strawberry Twizzler."

Akimi Hughes was giving Piya Sarkarati a heads-up about what to expect inside the Board Game Hall of Fame.

"Toughest. Game. Ever," she told her.

Dr. Zinchenko strode up to the microphone. "Very well. The meet and greet is officially over. It is time, once again, to pass out the lPads. Each of our four teams will visit eight exhibits, although no two teams will be on the same track through the museum. At the exhibits, you might engage in a game, parse a puzzle, or resolve a riddle."

"Oooh," said Mr. Lemoncello. "Lovely and luminous alliteration, Yanina."

"Thank you, sir." She turned back to the contestants. "You will need to find eight answers—each one a specific number of letters long. You will type those answers into your lPad. The letters to your answers will fill in the circular bubbles on your virtual answer sheet."

"Circular are the best kind of bubbles," said Mr. Lemoncello. "Personally, I can't stand a square bubble. Too edgy."

"Under some of the bubbles, you will see numbers. The letters inside those numbered bubbles will make up words in a seventy-six-letter phrase."

"Is it the same one Kyle and I had?" asked Akimi.

Dr. Zinchenko shook her head. "No."

"Darn."

"But wait," said Mr. Raymo, "there's more."

Mr. Lemoncello sighed. "There usually is."

"That seventy-six-letter phrase," Dr. Zinchenko continued, "will lead you to the ultimate and final answer."

"Whew," said Mr. Lemoncello, taking off his top hat and dabbing his brow. "This is more complicated than the recipe for primordial soup as written by the Scoundrels of Skullport!"

Dr. Zinchenko nodded. "Why is this game so difficult and challenging, you might ask?"

"Dr. Zinchenko?" said Haley, who knew a cue when she heard one. "Why is this game so difficult and challenging?"

"Because, as you will soon learn, the prize for winning is equally magnificent and marvelous."

"Mr. Lemoncello?" said Mr. Raymo, suddenly acting like a TV game show host. "Tell them what it is!"

Mr. Lemoncello smiled and held up both his arms spread wide.

There was an impish twinkle in his eye.

Finally, when the crowd was breathless with anticipation, he told them what the prize would be:

"Everything! Abso-tootly-lutely *EVERYTHING*!"

Mr. Lemoncello looked offstage.

"Maestro, if you please?"

Suddenly, the sound of sappy violins started to pour out of the outdoor loudspeakers, giving Mr. Lemoncello a very emotional musical track for his coming pronouncement.

"Ladies and gentlemen, boys and girls, buoys and gulls, as we celebrate our glorious past with this brand-new Board Game Hall of Fame, it's also time to think of the Future. As you may have noticed, every year, on my birthday, I grow older. And as I count those candles upon my cake, I ponder deep thoughts such as 'I hope I don't set off the smoke detector' and 'Can I lick the frosting off the candles now?' I also say to myself, 'Luigi, you are not going to be here forever. You only rented Chuck E. Cheese for two hours. And one day, sad to say, you won't be here at all. When you are gone, who will take over the Imagination Factory and the Gameworks Factory? Who will inherit your game-making empire and your bulging bazillion-dollar bank account? Who will fill your squeaking banana shoes?' "

The crowd gasped. So did most of the contestants lined up behind Mr. Lemoncello on the stage. They had never stopped to consider a world without Luigi L. Lemoncello in it.

Jack McClintock and his father, on the other hand, had. They talked all the time about what they would change at the factory if it were theirs. That's why they were both smirking, just a little.

"I have no children," Mr. Lemoncello continued, "except, of course, the millions of children all over the globe whom I have entertained with games, quick costume changes, and Lemonberry Fizz. I have no heir apparent, and soon I may go bald and have no hair apparent, either. No, my good friends. I just love making games and having fun. And so, it occurs to me that a younger version of me, someone who shares my love for puzzles and games and general silliness, could, one day—not too soon, hopefully—be the perfectly prepared person to take over all things Lemoncello.

"So, I have decided to host a series of games. A tournament of champions! The winner, or winners, of these contests will be awarded a titanium ticket that will grant them access to the ultimate, final, not to mention concluding round—the one game that will decide, once and for all, who, in the, as I said, very distant future, will take over my gaming empire and become richer than the King of Tokyo, King Oil, and the Merchant of Venus combined!"

Akimi's partner, Piya, gave her a confused look. "Huh?"

"They're games," Akimi whispered. "Mr. Lemoncello is all about the games."

"Oh . . ."

Mr. Lemoncello spun around to face the eight contestants. The weepy music was replaced by a snazzy game show theme.

"The first of the titanium tickets will be awarded right here tonight to someone from Hudson Hills. To my friends from Ohio, and, of course, Mario: Not to worry. You four will also have a chance to win the grand prize. Even though you are playing today in an advisory capacity, I am already plotting a similar gaming extravaganza for you and all the other members of the Lemoncello library's board. That will be your time to shine, exclamation point!"

"Cool," said Akimi. "I've always wanted to own a multinational game company."

"Me too," said Andrew.

"Me three," added Simon.

He'd *love* taking over Mr. Lemoncello's empire so he could create incredible new games like the ones he invented up in his attic.

Mr. Lemoncello turned back to the crowd.

"Good friends of Hudson Hills: Rest assured that whomsoever I choose to carry my name forward into the future will be someone fantabulous and awesometastic. Someone who will run things the way I would run them. Someone who will insure that your payday envelope always includes a candy bar of the same name. Someone who will solemnly swear that Taco Tuesdays in the company cafeteria shall be observed the way they were meant to be: with extra guacamole!"

The crowd shouted a collective "Woo-hoo!"

"So, over the next two hours, those are the stakes you four citizens of Hudson Hills, you sons and daughters of my beloved factory workers, shall be playing for: a chance to one day own everything in the global Lemoncello empire. Good luck to you all!"

More cheers from the crowd. Simon was clapping like crazy.

Mr. Lemoncello glanced down at his gold pocket watch.

"It is nearly six. When the clock in the museum's grand hall strikes the hour, pay very close attention. For that is when the big game truly begins!"

A clock chimed somewhere inside the Board Game Hall of Fame.

"Open the doors!" cried Mr. Lemoncello. "It's time for our contestants to visit the past, present, and future of board games!"

Mr. McClintock rushed toward the stage. His new set of keys—one for every lock in the Board Game Hall of Fame—jingled on the shiny new ring clipped to his belt.

"Out of my way. Coming through. Head of security. Coming through. Man with keys. Step aside."

He reached Jack. Dragged him away from the kid with the goggle glasses. Peckleman.

"Jack will be right back," Mr. McClintock snapped.

"But we're supposed to go inside right now," whined Peckleman. "Mr. Lemoncello opened the doors."

Mr. McClintock gave him his steeliest stare. "I said he'll be right back. Do I make myself clear, soldier?"

Peckleman looked like he might wet his pants. "Oh. Okay. See you inside, Jack." Peckleman ran through the open doors.

Mr. McClintock braced his hands on Jack's shoulders. "Son?"

"Yes, sir?"

"Take no prisoners in there. Victory belongs to the swift. This is our shot. You know how we talk about what we'd do if we were Mr. Lemoncello?"

"Yes, sir."

"Well, son, now we can be. Win that titanium ticket at all costs!"

"Don't worry, Dad. I'll do whatever it takes. No holds barred."

"That's my boy. Now go make me proud."

"Yes, sir. I'll also go make us rich!"

"Whoa!" said all eight contestants the instant they stepped through the towering twin doors and entered the Board Game Hall of Fame's four-story lobby.

It was a glistening atrium with banks of brightly colored elevators resembling bubble-tipped game pieces shooting up and down like rocket-propelled Hershey's Kisses. Projections of emoji, the stars of Mr. Lemoncello's Fantabulous Floating Emoji game, drifted across the walls, which were covered with enlarged game board art: box tops, advertising posters, and shelves displaying sculptures of famous tokens and playing pieces. Curling clear tubes, like something you'd see at a water park, snaked their way through the open area overhead.

A giant portrait of Mr. Lemoncello hanging on the wall sprang to holographic life.

"Welcome to the Board Game Hall of Fame! Have a great day and enjoy your stay, hey hey hey!"

"Thank you, sir!" Andrew shouted up at the talking painting.

"You're welcome, Andrew!" the Mr. Lemoncello in the oil painting shouted back.

There were columns of colorful game board boxes stacked on top of each other climbing up to the glass ceiling. The floor was tiled to look like Mr. Lemoncello's famous Cheesy Squeezy Pachisi board. An ornate grandfather clock, at least fifteen feet tall, stood against one wall, surrounded by framed antique game boards.

Simon peered up at the clock. It was fascinating, with frozen, hand-painted figurines of children at play. Simon could see two kids on a tilted seesaw, a juggling boy looking up at three suspended balls, a girl holding a balloon, and one boy in a top hat with a board game tucked under his arm who looked like a young Luigi Lemoncello. All of the miniature characters, with jointed marionette limbs, looked ready to spring into animated action the instant the clock struck its next full hour.

Simon would've loved to tear the clock apart to see how it worked.

"Welcome to the Board Game Hall of Fame," said the hologram of a portly man in a purple tailcoat. He looked around suspiciously. "Don't tell anybody, but I did it with the candlestick in the library."

"That's Professor Plum!" shouted Piya Sarkarati. "He's from a board game!"

"Um, they all are," Akimi told her partner.

"Help yourself to all the snacks and candy you like!" Professor Plum continued. "Feel free to play with your food."

There were crystal bowls filled with Mr. Lemoncello's Anagraham Crackers, Linking Licorice, and Squisheroo Marshmallow Building Blocks.

A parade of famous board game characters whirled its way through the atrium, all of the 3-D holograms waving at the contestants.

"Look, Simon," whispered Soraiya, "there's Rich Uncle Pennybags from Monopoly!"

Simon gulped.

Did Soraiya just call him Simon?

"Um, my name is Mario. . . ."

"I know." Soraiya was still whispering. Fortunately, the other three Hudson Hills contestants were off with their partners, playing with the snacks or pointing at the holograms. "So, does Mr. Lemoncello know you're doing this?"

"Doing, uh, what?" Simon put both hands on his hips and stuck out his chest. He was trying to act cool dudish, the way Haley had taught him.

"I recognized your eyes, Simon," Soraiya said with a smile. "Nobody else's are that green."

"Actually, they're hazel. . . ."

"Are we cheating right now?"

Simon shook his head. "No. I can't win. They just wanted someone to fill in for Kyle Keeley. He's sick. Some kind of stomach flu."

"Well, I'm glad they picked you. There's nobody else I'd rather play with. Check it out!" She pointed at a jolly red polar bear. "He's from Don't Break the Ice. And there's Gramma Nutt and the princess from Candy Land!"

"Cool," said Simon. Since his grandfather never let him play board games, he had no idea who any of these characters might be. He touched Soraiya's elbow. "You sure you're okay with this? They told me Mr. Lemoncello would be."

Soraiya nodded. "I'll be even more okay with it if we win! Oooh, gross. Stay away from that guy!"

A big plastic head, rumbling around on wheels like a float in a parade, cruised through the atrium. It was at least ten feet tall and sculpted to look like a young guy with an awkward smile, a cowlick flip to his waxy black hair, and nubby bumps all over his face.

"That's Pimple Pete," said Soraiya. "That red dot on the tip of his nose? It's an exploding mega zit!"

"Really?"

"Yeah. It's gross."

Several plastic bumper-car-sized cars, a minibus, and a white ice cream truck scooted around the room. "Those are from Rush Hour," Soraiya explained.

Simon was relaxing a little. He was relieved that he

didn't have to pretend to be someone he wasn't around his friend.

Another plastic character rolled into the room. This one had a bright-red nose, an apple for an Adam's apple, and butterflies in its stomach.

"Who's that?" Simon asked.

"Cavity Sam," said Soraiya. "From Operation! It's a classic."

"Hey," Jack called out. "Does anybody know—is this parade part of the game?"

"Probably not," said his partner, Andrew, tapping their lPad. "There's nothing on this stupid screen except nothing."

A panel in the glass ceiling opened and a hydraulic lift slowly lowered a very large egg timer.

"All right, contestants, may I have your attention, please?" Mr. Lemoncello's voice echoed out of speakers planted all around the room. "We have put exactly two hours' worth of sand into that timer. I should know. I counted the grains myself. When it tips over, your lPads will illuminate and tell you where to find your first item in this seriously stupendous scavenger hunt through our brain-boggling new hall of fame. Remember: No two teams will be following the exact same path. You might go to an exhibit that nobody else visits. Or you may go to one with all the other teams."

Dr. Zinchenko took over the narration. "Your lPad tablets will present you with your virtual answer sheets.

As you pick up letters at each exhibit, you will simultaneously start building a seventy-six-letter phrase. That phrase will be your key to finding the titanium ticket. A floor plan of the museum will also be available to you on your device."

"Oh, boy," said Mr. Lemoncello as the two-hour timer started to slowly tip over. "It's time. On your mark! Get set! Lemon, cello, go!"

All four IPads *DING*ed at the same time.

Simon and Soraiya looked down at their device and read what was scrolling across the screen: *His life was very checkered. To find out more, visit Famous Game Makers on the second floor.*

"Elevator or stairs?" said Soraiya.

Simon looked over to the elevator banks. The other players were taking turns jabbing the up button repeatedly.

"Stairs!"

They raced to the steps, which were made out of thick glass planks in a rainbow of colors like the keys on Simon's glockenspiel. They bounded up the stairs. Every step produced a higher note on the musical scale.

"It *is* like my glockenspiel!" said Simon.

"So, who's our famous game maker?" asked Soraiya,

when they reached the landing at the staircase's halfway point.

"I don't know. I think we just need to do what the clue says. Go up to the second floor and find this Famous Game Makers exhibit."

"Sounds good to me," said Soraiya. "But, Simon?"

"Yeah?"

"Your nose is wobbling."

"Haley made it out of rubber for me."

Soraiya laughed. "Reminds me of that wobbler you plucked out of the Kujenga tower!"

Simon laughed, too. "I just hope it doesn't start blinking."

They reached the top of the stairs (it was a high C).

Soraiya, who was carrying the team's lPad, showed its display to Simon.

"There must be a GPS tracker inside the device," she said. "That dot? That's us. Now, where are the Famous Game Makers?"

"Calculating route," said the lPad (which sounded like Dr. Zinchenko).

A jagged line appeared on the screen.

Soraiya took off running. "Follow me!"

Simon trotted as fast as he could. He didn't want his disguise to fall off. Soraiya might be fine with the truth about "Mario." He doubted Jack McClintock would feel the same way.

"There!" said Soraiya, pointing to an illuminated sign. "Famous Game Makers."

"And there!" shouted Simon, pointing to an antique game board displayed in a glass case.

It looked like a red-and-white checkerboard. Some white spaces had good things like "Bravery," "Industry," and "Fame" printed on them. Others had bad things like "Crime," "Prison," and "Ruin" stamped on them.

"Check out the box top!" said Soraiya, pointing to another display case. "The Checkered Game of Life, by Milton Bradley Company, Springfield, Mass. It fits the clue perfectly!"

"This was Milton Bradley's very first game," said Simon, reading the wall plaque. "Created in 1860, when he was just twenty-three years old. It came back as the Game of Life in 1960."

"The one with the cars and the pink and blue peg people," said Soraiya. "Let's see if it fits."

Soraiya swiped right, and a new image filled the lPad screen:

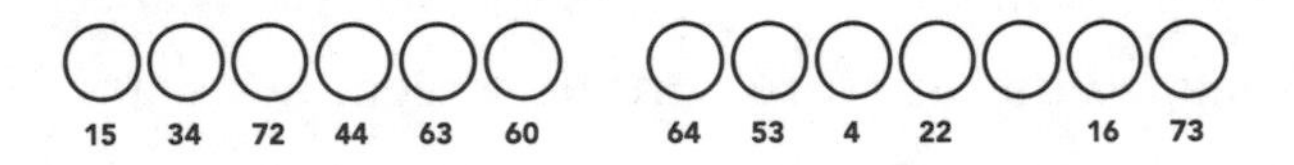

"It's a two-word answer," she said. "Six letters. Seven letters."

"Milton Bradley!" said Simon.

Soraiya tapped the keyboard, typing in M-I-L-T-O-N B-R-A-D-L-E-Y.

When she hit return, the lPad made a very pleasant *GA-LING-PA-TING!* sound, signaling that the answer was correct. Next, the screen did an animated transition to a new visual and the twelve numbered letters plopped into their assigned spaces in a seventy-six-letter phrase:

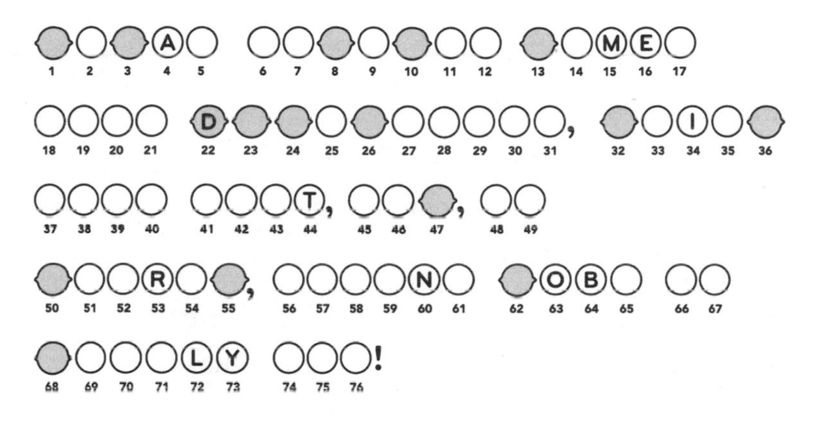

"Yes!" said Soraiya. "We're on our way!"

"We definitely are," said Simon.

"Huh. I wonder why some of the circles look like lemons," said Soraiya. "See? Check out number twenty-two, where our 'D' went."

Simon stared at the screen. "I have a feeling those lemony letters will, when the phrase is all filled in, help us find Mr. Lemoncello's titanium ticket."

"Of course. Well done, Simon . . . I mean, Mario!"

"You're right! You should call me Mario. Just in case Carolyn, Piya, or Jack hears us talking."

"Yeah," said Soraiya. "Especially Jack."

"Where to next?"

Soraiya tapped the IPad screen. The image of the seventy-six-letter phrase shook itself clear like an Etch A Sketch. Up came the next scavenger hunt clue.

This one was a rebus.

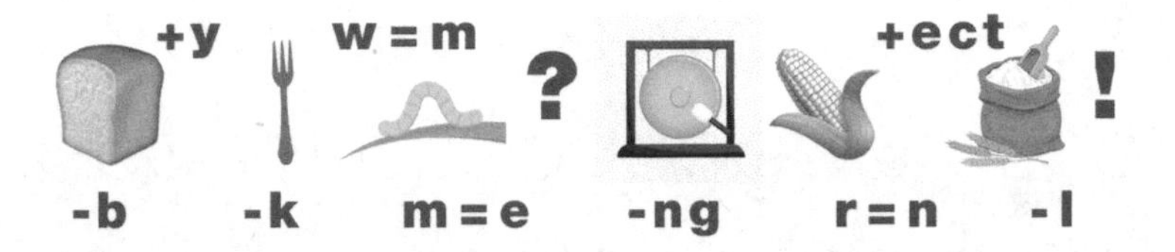

"Oh, man," said Soraiya, loud enough for anybody on the second floor to hear. "I wish my friend Simon Skrindle was here. He's excellent at these picture puzzles. Best I've ever seen."

Simon grinned. "Why, thank you," he whispered.

"Me? I'm terrible at these things. I mean, what's that picture at the end? Some kind of sack?"

"I'm pretty sure that's a sack of flour. So we take away the 'L' and add an exclamation point, giving us 'four!' "

Soraiya made a rolling circle gesture. "Keep going, Mario."

Simon hummed a little ditty to help him think, studied the puzzle, and gave Soraiya the answer. "It says, 'Ready for more? Go connect four!' Of course, I have no idea what four we're supposed to connect. . . ."

"It's another board game!" said Soraiya. "Connect Four. It's a two-player game. You pick a color, red or yellow, and take turns dropping one disc at a time into a plastic grid."

"So, where do we find Connect Four?" said Simon.

"Upstairs," said the navigator voice from the lPad. "Third floor."

"Let's go," said Soraiya, seeing an empty elevator. She and Simon hopped into the waiting car.

"Wait a second," said Simon as they slowly ascended. "If it's a two-player game, does that mean I have to play you?"

Soraiya shrugged. "I guess. Maybe."

The elevator *DING*ed and the doors slid open.

"There you are!" shouted Jack McClintock.

"Took you two long enough," whined his partner, Andrew Peckleman.

"What's the matter, Mario?" Jack sneered. "Did you guys have trouble finding your first answer?"

"We're on our third," said Andrew proudly. "But our stupid lPad keeps telling us to 'wait here' until our opponents arrive."

"Are you guys playing Connect Four?" asked Soraiya.

"Yep," said Jack. "Against you two!"

Lights dimmed and the panels surrounding the Connect Four exhibit were filled with grainy, washed-out images from what was labeled as a "1977 Television Commercial."

A brother and sister with strange hairdos slid discs into a seven-column, six-row, vertically suspended grid.

"Object?" said the commercial's announcer. "Connect four of your checkers in a row while preventing your opponent from doing the same! But, look out—your opponent can sneak up on you and win the game! Connect Four. The vertical checkers game!"

A panel in the floor popped open and a mammoth Connect Four game rose up. It was at least ten feet tall and twelve feet wide. Next, two circular panels in the floor slid open and up rose two columns of stacked colored discs—each one the size of a pizza pan.

"These aren't so heavy," said Simon with his best Mario 'tude. He picked up a couple. "Now, how do we drop 'em down the slots?"

"Easy," said Jack. "You have to scale the wall, bro."

"Cool," said Simon.

"Show him how it's done, Jack," said Andrew.

Jack grabbed a yellow disc, tucked it under his arm, and climbed up the giant game board, using the rims of the open circles for handholds and footholds.

He dropped the yellow disc into the middle slot. It slid down to the bottom row.

"I've got this, Mario," said Soraiya.

"You want me to heave the discs up to you?" said Simon.

"Yeah. That'd be great."

Soraiya scurried up the side of the game board and dropped a red disc down a column.

"Hand me up another disc, Andy!" shouted Jack.

"Um, no one really calls me 'Andy,' " said Andrew.

"Now they do. Come on. Move it."

Andrew grunted and tried to hoist the thick yellow disc up to Jack.

"Never mind," said Jack, scampering down to grab the plastic circle from Andrew. "You need to work on your upper-body strength."

Andrew just nodded.

Jack scaled the game grid again and dropped another disc down another slot.

"Here you go, partner," said Simon. He passed the next red disc up to Soraiya. She dropped it down a slot and instantly blocked Jack's attempt to do four in a row across the bottom of the game board.

The game continued. It reminded Simon of tic-tac-toe, a game that was impossible to win if both sides knew how to play.

But then, Jack pulled a very cunning, very strategic move that forced Soraiya to block his horizontal *and* vertical lines of four but ended up giving him four in a row on the diagonal!

"Oh, man," said Soraiya.

"We win!" said Andrew.

"You mean *I* win," said Jack, leaping off the game board.

"We're a team, Jack."

"Maybe. But I'm the only one playing for the titanium ticket, Andy!"

"True . . ."

"Did a riddle pop up on the lPad?"

"Yes," said Andrew. "It's very simple." He was about to read it out loud.

"Andrew?" warned Jack, shaking his head. "Don't be an I-D ten-T."

"A what?"

"An idiot! That's *our* clue, not *theirs*."

"Okay, okay," said Andrew. "You know, I'm the one

who's won a few Lemoncello games. I'm supposed to be the one coaching you."

"Just type in the answer if you know it, Andy."

Andrew jabbed the glass screen of his lPad. "Oh. Nice. It gave us a bunch of letters in the phrase."

"Great. Where to next?"

"The library!" Andrew said excitedly. "Now, in the library, you *should* listen to me. I was second-in-command for the Alexandriaville Middle School Library Aides Society."

"Whatever," said Jack. "Where's the library?"

"First floor."

The teammates took off, leaving Simon and Soraiya to stare at the yellow-and-red configuration of their losing Connect Four game. The sound of chirping crickets came out of the ceiling speakers.

"So, uh, now what?" wondered Soraiya.

"Good question!" thundered Mr. Lemoncello's voice. "Jiminy, how did all these crickets hop into my sound-proof booth? Shoo! Now then, Soraiya and, uh, Mario, you have a choice. One, you can wait for another team to come along and try to beat *them* at Connect Four—even though there is no guarantee that this particular exhibit will be a stop on any of the other teams' scavenger hunt paths. Or . . ."

"Yes?" said Soraiya. "What's our 'or'?"

"Something you might use to row a boat. It might also

be a naturally occurring mineral. Or, it might even be a different kind of Connect Four puzzle."

"We'll take the new puzzle!" said Simon. "If, you know, that's okay with you, Soraiya."

She nodded. "It's what I would've said, too, Coach."

Now they just had to wait for Mr. Lemoncello to tell them what kind of game they'd be playing next!

"Oh, are you waiting for me to tell you what kind of game to play next?" said Mr. Lemoncello.

"Yes, sir," Soraiya and Simon said together.

"Very well, here is your second Connect Four puzzle," said Mr. Lemoncello.

The nine discs in the center of the Connect Four grid—some red, some yellow—began to blend together and glow orange.

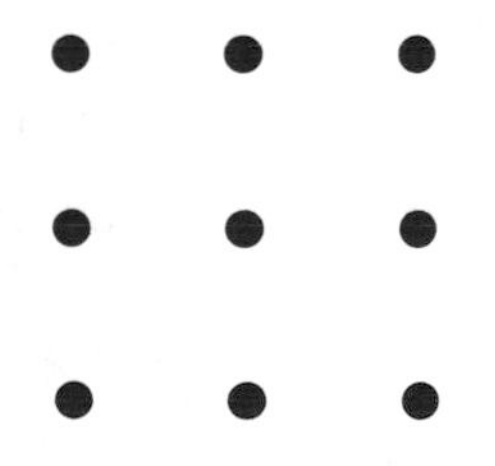

"Your challenge?" said Mr. Lemoncello. "*Connect* these nine orange dots using only *four* lines."

"That's impossible," mumbled Soraiya.

"Not really," said Simon. "We just need to look at the problem in a different way.

"When you think you have your answer," instructed Mr. Lemoncello, "swipe a finger over the playing pieces and your motion will generate a red line. Remember, you can only use four lines to connect all nine dots."

Simon hummed to himself and focused on the puzzle for maybe half a minute.

"Okay," he said when the answer clicked in his head. "Here's one way to do it."

He dragged his hand across the game board, venturing outside the limits created by the square of nine dots.

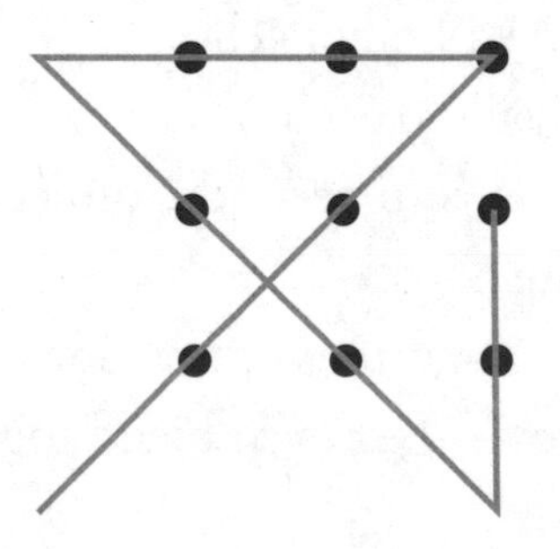

"Or," he said, wiping his hand back and forth like an eraser to clear the lines, "while we're at it, how about this?"

He drew another connected four lines.

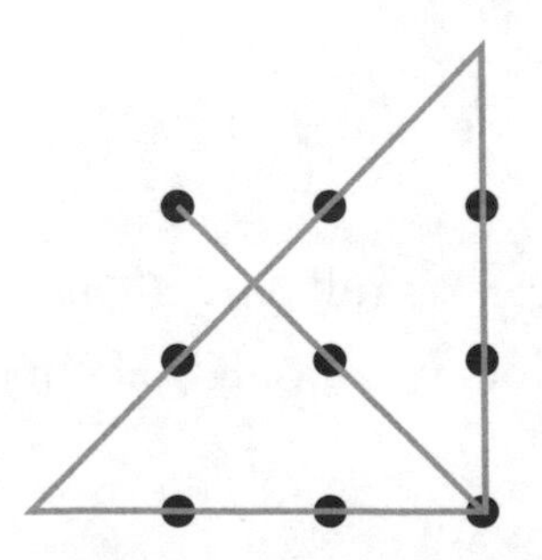

Soraiya clapped. Simon laughed.

"You are awesome, Mario!" said Soraiya.

And Simon actually felt like he was. Faking that he was the confident Mario was making him feel, well, confident.

"How about another one?" he said, swiping his hand across the board, creating four new red lines.

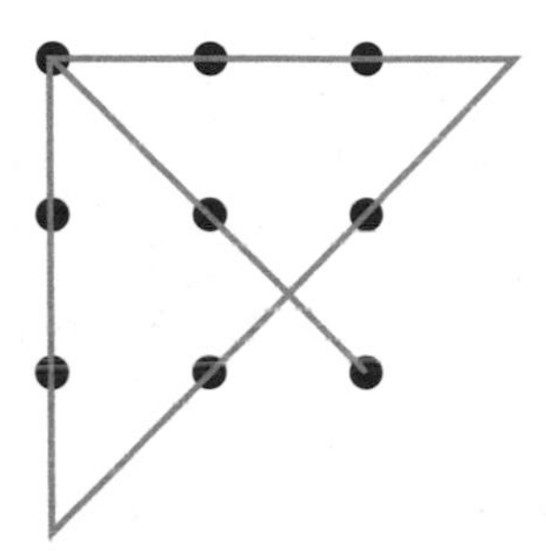

Now Soraiya was laughing.

"One more," said Simon, with a boatload of confidence. Only this time, it wasn't because he was pretending to be Mario. This time it was because he knew he was good at seeing things other people sometimes didn't. He could deconstruct the pattern of dots and imagine new lines connecting them. "This time, I'll use only *three* lines."

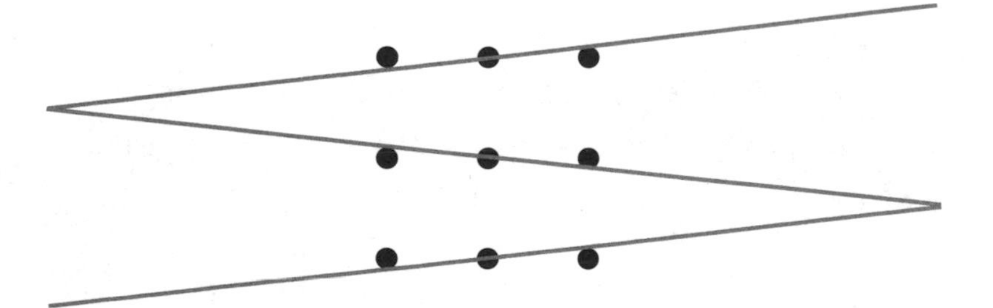

"Congratulicitations!" boomed Mr. Lemoncello's voice. "By doing more than was required, you have left me feeling inspired. You have also earned . . ."

There was a loud *DING-DING-DING!*

A rubbery playing card shot up from the floor as if it had been ejected from a toaster.

Soraiya grabbed it in midair.

"What is it?" asked Simon.

"Some kind of bendable bonus card!" said Soraiya, showing it to Simon. It had the word **BONUS** written in big, bold letters on each side. It was also made out of thin rubber and sort of floppy.

"What's it good for?" Simon wondered aloud.

"It's a bendable bonus card!" said Mr. Lemoncello. "Save it until you really need it and, then, use it wisely."

"Um, okay," said Simon.

"Don't worry, Mr. L," said Soraiya, sliding the rubbery card into her pocket. "We will!"

"Toodle-oo!" said Mr. Lemoncello. "Play on! Lemoncello, out!"

"What's on the lPad now?" asked Simon.

"A very Lemoncello-ish question. 'What would you call a similar game with one large pancake?' "

"How many words?"

"Two. Seven letters. Three letters. And every single letter is numbered. That means they all move into the seventy-six-letter phrase. This is big, Mario!"

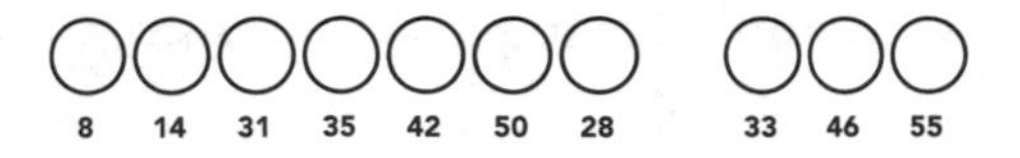

Simon tapped out a glockenspiel tune in his head to help him think.

"Aha! 'Connect One'! You just drop one pancake into the grid and win."

When the letter bubbles were all filled, the screen dissolved into a progress report on the seventy-six-letter build:

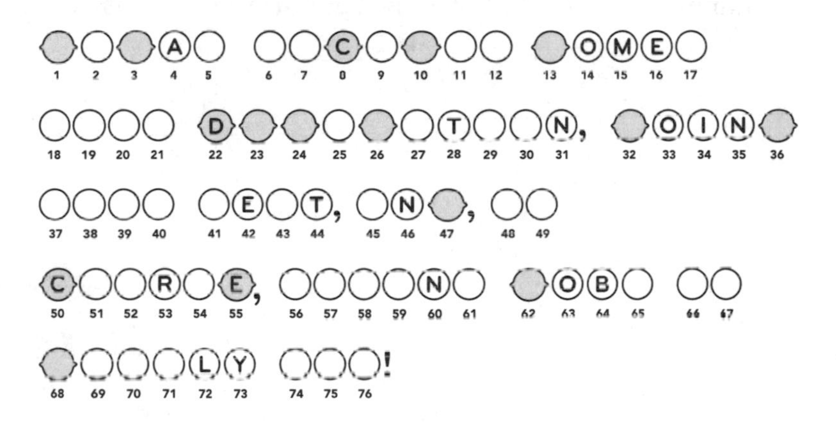

"We picked up a few more lemony letters!" said Soraiya.

"Fantastic," said Simon.

"Now we just have to figure out what they mean."

"True. But first we have to move on to our next exhibit."

"Right," said Soraiya. "And, Mario?"

"Yeah?"

"Fix your wig. It's kind of lopsided."

"Gotcha!" Simon adjusted his hair while Soraiya tapped the screen. Up came a clue for their next destination.

" 'Strategy time. Go!' "

"That's it?" said Simon.

"It's all we need."

"Seriously?"

Soraiya laughed. "Mr. Lemoncello is going old school on us. This game was one of my dad's favorites when he was a kid. So, he taught me how to play it. It's called Stratego!"

Simon finally got it. "Strategy, go! Stra-tee-go!"

"Exactly. So, come on. Let's *go*!"

"Stratego is located on the first floor," the IPad told Soraiya and Simon.

"Let's take the steps instead of the elevator," suggested Soraiya. "Maybe we can see how everybody else is doing."

"Good idea!" said Simon.

They headed for the staircase. On the way down, the steps played "Heart and Soul."

"Hey," said Simon, "do you think Jack bought my Mario act?"

"Totally. Because pretending to be somebody else is letting you be who you are."

"Huh?"

"You're good at these games and riddles. You always have been. When you're Mario, you let yourself have fun being clever. You don't hold back."

"I don't come off too braggy?"

"Shh. There's Haley and Carolyn. And that game is called Mr. Lemoncello's Krazy Karaoke Dance and Sing Thing!"

The two girls were matching dance steps on the arcade game's glowing floor pads while singing a song, karaoke-style.

"Let's do another one!" said Carolyn when the song-and-dance routine ended. "How about 'Every Good Boy Deserves Fudge'?"

"But we already earned our next clue," coached Haley.

Carolyn shrugged. "So? I don't really want to own a game-making factory when I grow up. I want to be on TV like you! Let's dance the Fudgsicle!"

"Oh-kay," said Haley. She tapped a button on the video console's control panel and they started singing and dancing again.

"Come on," Soraiya whispered. "I think Carolyn has basically taken herself out of the competition. She got her prize. Meeting Haley."

"So it's just you, Jack, and Piya," said Simon.

They hurried down the steps to the second floor. Now the piano steps plinked out "Chopsticks." Sweat dribbled from under the webbed lining of Simon's wig. It tickled his ears and neck.

On the second floor, they saw Akimi and Piya playing an oversized version of Rock 'Em Sock 'Em Robots. The towering remote-controlled red and blue bots were inside a roped-off, official-sized boxing ring.

"I'm gonna knock your block off!" shouted Akimi, pushing a button on her controller that made the blue robot jab an uppercut at the red robot's blocky head.

"Ha! Missed!" cried Piya, bobbing and weaving to avoid the blow.

"Well, one of us has to win or we'll never get our clue!" said Akimi.

"Don't look at me," said Piya, punching a button to land another punch. "I'm not taking a fall!"

"Me neither!"

"Looks like they're both way too into the game," Soraiya whispered. "Guess that's the danger of hosting a scavenger hunt inside a hall of fame that is basically a mammoth Dave and Buster's. Too many distractions."

"Fine, Piya!" they heard Akimi shout behind them. "Knock my block off. We need to wrap up our third riddle!"

"Third?" Simon whispered to Soraiya. "We've only done two!"

"Yeah. Losing that first Connect Four game slowed us down. But, like Kyle Keeley always says, 'the game is never over until it's over.' "

Mr. McClintock was in his security surveillance control room, where the fifty new screens linked to closed-circuit cameras inside the Board Game Hall of Fame were all glowing.

He was observing the kids on their scavenger hunt as it neared the end of its first hour. There was no sound, so he couldn't hear what anybody was saying. But he could watch them.

Jack had been doing great, despite being teamed up with Andrew, the weak-kneed whiner from Ohio.

Akimi Hughes and Piya Sarkarati were hot on his heels. They'd finally wrapped up their Rock 'Em Sock 'Em Robots bout and had moved on to a railroad train game called Ticket to Ride. And yes, Mr. Lemoncello and his imagineers had installed an actual miniature ride-along railroad on the fourth floor.

Carolyn Hudson seemed more interested in singing, dancing, and Haley Daley than in winning. She wasn't a serious threat and wouldn't be going home with the McClintocks' titanium ticket.

Jack's other competition was the plant manager's daughter, Soraiya Mitchell, and her partner, the super-gamer Mario. The kid with the floppy black mop top was good.

While Akimi and Piya were slowing down (it takes time to build a transcontinental railroad), Soraiya and Mario were easily winning their Napoleonic battle on the first floor.

The forty Stratego pieces they played with looked like castle towers with turrets. Mr. Lemoncello and his imagineers had somehow made it so the chunky playing pieces, each one about two and a half feet tall, could whir and scoot around a game board that covered the entire floor of a room. Flat, flickering images of soldiers from the Napoleonic Wars were animated on the backs of the oversized playing pieces.

Soraiya and Mario won their battle in record time. Probably because Mario rigged up what amounted to a domino drop and toppled most of the enemy red bricks in an extremely clever, well-orchestrated move.

The leader of the triumphant blue bricks made some kind of speech, then nobly bowed. When he did, the rest of his army lined up and zipped an illuminated riddle across their blocks like you'd see on a digital reader board:

SMALL WAS MY STATURE, BUT MY SUCCESS WAS GREAT.
UNTIL I ENTERED BELGIUM TO BE HANDED MY FATE.

Mr. McClintock watched Soraiya scan the team's tablet device.

They needed an eight-letter answer.

"Napoleon," Mr. McClintock mumbled, one second before Soraiya tapped in that answer. Mr. McClintock toggled a lever to make the overhead camera zoom in on Soraiya's lPad. Five of the eight letters from NAPOLEON flew into the seventy-six-letter phrase. One of them landed in the third circle, which was a lemon:

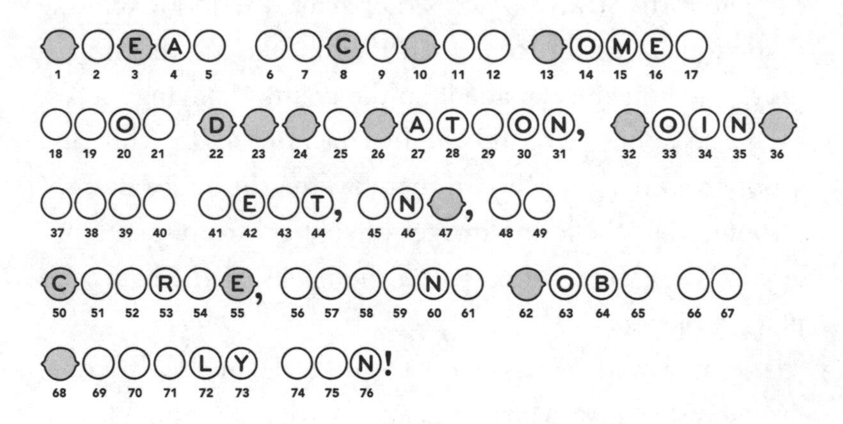

Meanwhile, in the second-floor theater, Jack and his partner, Andrew Peckleman, were having trouble deciphering Mr. Lemoncello's Fantabulous Floating Emoji as they were projected on the movie screen.

"Come on, Jack!" grumbled Mr. McClintock, watching

his son struggle. "This is baby stuff. The category is nursery rhymes!"

Up came another puzzle.

It should've been easy.

But neither Jack nor Andrew could figure it out!

If Jack didn't win, that meant Mr. McClintock and his son would never get to take over Mr. Lemoncello's entire empire and become bajillionaires!

And that, he thought, *is one hundred percent unacceptable.*

"I hate these stupid rebuses!" whined Andrew.

"Stand aside, Peckleman," said Jack. "I've got this."

He studied the string of images one more time:

"I know this one!" he said. "It's 'The Old Man and the Sheep'!"

"The Farmers' Almanac," blurted Andrew.

"That's not a nursery rhyme!"

"Neither is 'The Old Man and the Sheep'! That's not even a real book!"

Jack hoped his father wasn't watching this soup sandwich on the CCTV monitors back home in the guardhouse.

"Why does the farmer look old?" fumed Andrew.

"Because 'Old MacDonald Had a Farm'!" said Jack.

Finally, bells rang and lights twirled. They had guessed correctly.

Another nursery rhyme rebus floated into view.

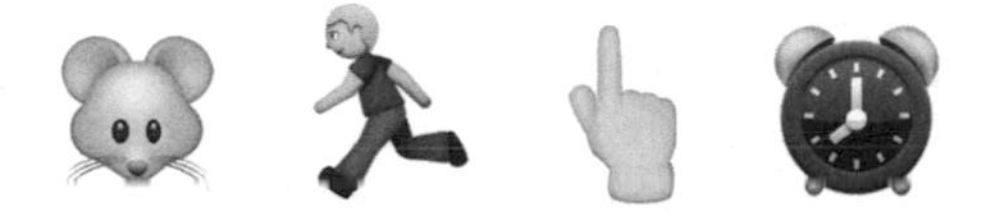

" 'The Rats of Narnia'!" blurted Jack.

"That's not a nursery rhyme, either," said Andrew.

" 'Three Blind Mice'!" said Jack.

"There's only one mouse in the puzzle!" sighed Andrew. "And it looks like it wants to run up a clock."

" 'Hickory Dickory Dock'!" said Jack. "The mouse ran up the clock."

More bells and swirling lights.

"How many more of these are there?" asked Andrew.

"Three," said Jack. "But then we get to go play Battleship."

"Oh, joy," sighed Andrew.

Meanwhile, Soraiya and Simon were heading to the basement.

"According to the floor plan," said Soraiya, "that's where we'll find Candy Crush Hour."

"Is that a real game?" asked Simon.

"It's a hybrid," said Soraiya, reading the notes on the

museum map. "It's 'all the brain-puzzling fun of Rush Hour combined with the whimsical magic of Candy Land.' "

"Oh-kay," said Simon, who wasn't familiar with either game. "What's Rush Hour?"

"You're basically in a traffic jam and have to slide trucks and cars and buses around to clear a path to the exit for your vehicle."

"And Candy Land?"

"It's for little kids. You race around Candy Cane Forest and the Gumdrop Mountains. You want to avoid the Molasses Swamp."

"I wonder how Mr. Lemoncello mixed the two games together?" said Simon.

He and Soraiya soon found out.

"The game grid is filled with melted molasses?" said Soraiya when they reached the exhibit and smelled the thick, treacly scent of sugarcane boiled down to a syrup.

"Is that brown goop on the floor molasses?" asked Simon.

"Yep. And we have to move that red car over there out of this mess. See the exit?"

Simon nodded. "We're gonna need to slide all these other vehicles out of the way first."

"And," said Soraiya, "the only way to do that is to hike through the swamp."

Simon gestured to a bench that looked like it was made out of a bent sheet of blue, pink, and yellow Dots candy. "Guess that's why there're two pairs of snow boots under that bench."

"So," said Soraiya as they sat down to slip on the rubbery galoshes, "are you still glad you're Mario today?"

"Hey, we're a team. Not even molasses can slow us down!"

Simon and Soraiya stepped over the curb and into the gooey glop.

"What's our play?" asked Soraiya.

Simon studied the arrangement of the very bright plastic vehicles, all about the size of bumper cars, trapped in the molasses.

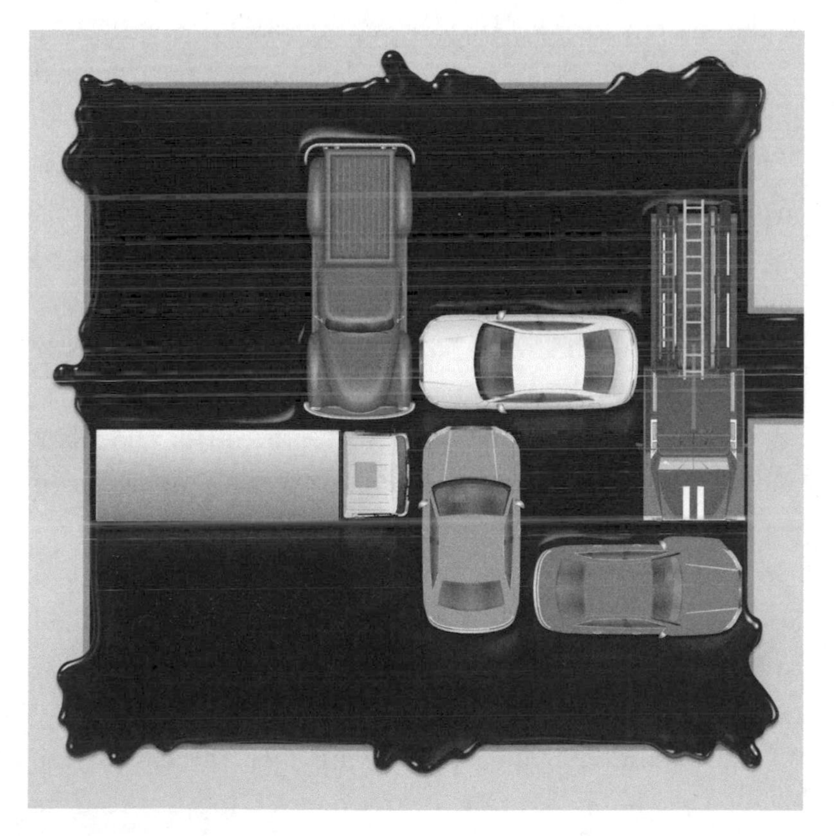

Simon tapped out a silent melody on his thighs as he studied the board. Once again, he saw things that other people might not.

"Okay. It's going to take sixteen moves. I'll drive the green car south to the wall while you back up the fire truck to the top."

"Got it!" said Soraiya.

The gluey syrup was up to their ankles and, with every step, it tried to suck the boots off their feet.

"This is disgusting!" shouted Soraiya, making her way to the fire truck.

Their feet made all sorts of rude noises as they slogged through the sticky bog.

"I'm in!" said Soraiya. "Guess what? The truck's steering wheel is a chocolate-covered pretzel. With sprinkles."

"Mine is the top of a lollipop," said Simon as he climbed into the little green car. "Find the accelerator pedal."

"You mean this thing that looks like an angled candy bar on the floor?"

"I guess so," said Simon, his mouth full of chocolate and crunchy chunks of candy cane. "Mine's made out of peppermint bark."

After the first two moves were made, Simon talked Soraiya through six more while he made seven. They had to slog through the sludge and climb into every vehicle at least once.

When Simon hauled himself up into the cab of the blue truck, he pulled down on a licorice loop to toot its air horn. It felt awesome to be up so high in the big rig's driver's seat.

After fifteen moves, the little red car had a clear path to the exit. Simon and Soraiya hopped out of their vehicles and sloshed through the icky brown muck, ready to ride the red car out of the swamp.

They were nearly there when suddenly a fudgy, sludgy creature sprang up from the gluey lagoon.

Startled, Simon almost fell backward into the molasses.

Some kind of gloppy monster that looked like the poop emoji's cousin was two feet in front of him. The thing was a lumpy mound of half-melted chocolate with a cherry-red tongue and the yellow candy eyes of a chocolate Easter bunny. It was also, for some reason, holding a Fudgsicle.

"That's Gloppy!" shouted Soraiya. "Give him a hug!"

"What?" cried Simon.

"He may look like a monster, but according to the official Candy Land website, 'He's really a lovable glop of chocolaty goo.' "

That surprised Simon. "You've been to the Candy Land website?"

"It was my favorite game when I was three years old. Gloppy gets lonely sitting in this swamp all by himself. Hug him."

"What?"

"Hug Gloppy!"

"Why don't you do it?"

"You're closer."

"Okay, okay."

Closing his eyes, Simon leaned forward and wrapped his arms around the animatronic, chocolate-dribbling creature. When he did, some kind of hydraulics whooshed and pulled the clicking-clacking monster mannequin down into the floor. The six-inch sea of syrupy molasses followed Gloppy down the sinkhole in a gurgling whirlpool of brown.

"Woo-hoo!" shouted Soraiya. "You drained the swamp. That'll make it a lot easier to roll the red car out of here."

"Let's do it!" said Simon. The front of his shirt and pants were smeared with fudge sludge. It was very tasty. Fortunately, none of the goop had splattered on his fake nose or rubber chin.

"Look," said Soraiya as she climbed into the passenger seat. "There's a pair of clean tracksuits in the back. We can change out of these dirty clothes."

"Let's drive out of here first."

"Good idea."

Simon grabbed the Peppermint Pattie steering wheel and pressed down on the accelerator (this one was made out of peanut brittle). The red car scooted across the molasses-free parking lot and out the exit slot. When it was clear of the curb, a trumpet fanfare blared out of its radio while a confetti shower of sprinkles and jimmies fell from the ceiling.

"That was a blast!" hollered Simon.

"Yeet!" said Soraiya as she showed Simon how to fist bump.

While they laughed, a digital message zipped across the tiny car's dashboard video screen.

"It's our next riddle!" said Soraiya.

It was a short one:

WHO IS GLOPPY?

"How many words in the answer?" asked Simon as Soraiya swiped her finger across their lPad to wake it up.

"Eight," reported Soraiya. "And one has an apostrophe!"

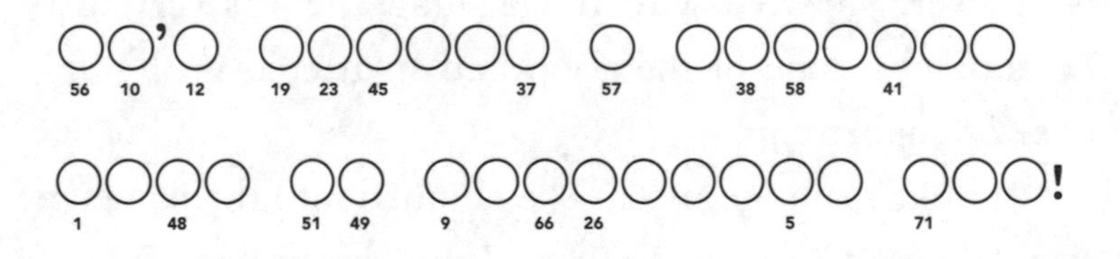

Soraiya slugged Simon playfully on the shoulder. "Ha! Now aren't you glad I went to the Candy Land website?"

She typed in the answer without missing a beat: *He's really a lovable glop of chocolaty goo!*

The screen dissolved into the seventy-six-letter phrase and automatically filled in twenty more circles:

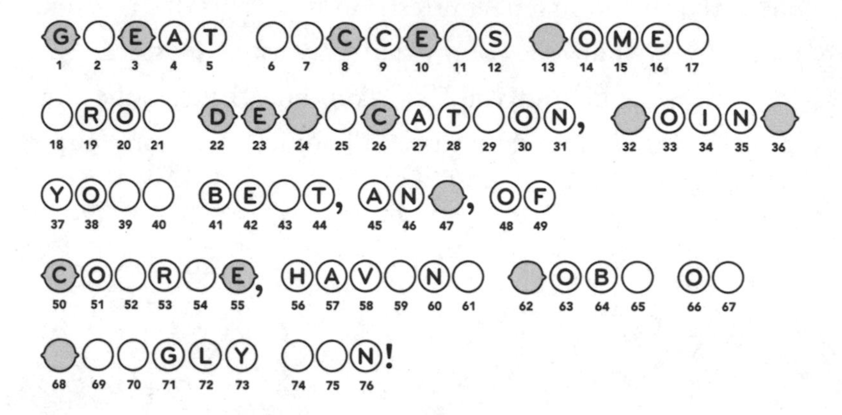

"Whoa," said Simon. "This is like the longest version of hangman ever played. But, I'm starting to see some words. 'Great.' 'Dedication.' Maybe 'success' . . ."

"We need to move on to the next game."

"There's a pair of changing booths over there," said Simon.

They grabbed the clean clothes, jumped out of the little red car, and dashed over to the tents.

"Where do we go next?" Simon yelled once he was inside his changing booth.

"A game that rhymes with rattle-hip!" Soraiya called from hers.

"Um, cattle-lip?"

Soraiya was silent. For five full seconds. "For a supergamer, you really don't play many board games, do you?"

"Just the ones I make up."

"Well," said Soraiya as she and Simon both stepped

out of the changing tents in fresh clothes, “this one is called Battleship! It’s another of my dad’s favorites. Come on.”

“I’m right behind you,” said Simon. “I just hope this battleship isn’t floating in a sea of something worse than molasses!”

Mr. McClintock watched Soraiya and Mario race out of the Candy Crush Hour room and head to the Battleship exhibit.

He glanced over to monitor number thirteen to check in on Haley Daley and Carolyn Hudson. It seemed they were finally tired of singing karaoke and doing dance routines. Zooming in on their iPad, Mr. McClintock discovered that Haley and Carolyn were slated to play Battleship, too.

"That means they'll be going up against Soraiya and Mario," Mr. McClintock mumbled, making notes on the legal pad he used to track the players' positions.

Jack and Andrew were still stuck in the nursery rhyme zone, wrestling with a final floating emoji rebus:

Frustrated, Mr. McClintock covered his face with his hands.

"It's 'rub-a-dub-dub, three men in a tub'!" he muttered, and realized that when Jack was a baby, he probably should've read him fewer bedtime stories about famous battles and more nursery rhymes.

Upstairs on the fourth floor, Akimi and Piya remained bogged down, hooking up a caboose to their choo-choo train.

If things stayed the way they were, Soraiya and Mario were going to win.

Unless something slowed *them* down, too.

Mr. McClintock stood up from the control desk and headed for the door. He needed to be Oscar Mike, on the move. He needed to leave his gingerbread house command post and do something, *anything* that might give Jack and Andrew an edge when they finally emerged from their struggle with the floating emoji.

Mr. McClintock had no idea what that something might be.

But it was time to go looking for it!

Simon and Soraiya found the Battleship exhibit.

A yellow submarine was docked near the side of a large indoor pool under a steamy atrium. Gentle waves rippled across the water.

"Good," said Soraiya. "No more syrup."

"Is the water gross?" asked Haley Daley as she and Carolyn Hudson drifted into the room. "Because these shoes are brand-new. Oh, hi, Mario. How's it going?"

Simon didn't answer. For half a second, he forgot who he was supposed to be. When he remembered, he puffed up his chest and thrust out his fake chin.

"I'm awesome, Hales," he said. "How you two doin'?" He tried to say it like a cool guy he'd seen on TV once.

"Groovy. Carolyn doesn't really care about inheriting Mr. Lemoncello's factory."

"I'd rather go to Hollywood and make movies,"

Carolyn explained. "It's why I'm glad I met Haley. It's why I tried so hard at the sidewalk board game."

"Carolyn's a smart and driven young woman," Haley said with a wink. "Just like me."

"So, Mario," said Carolyn, "do you go to the same middle school in Ohio that Haley used to go to?"

"Um, yes. I think so."

"Uh-oh, wait a second," said Haley, studying the yellow submarine bobbing in the water. "Are we supposed to climb inside that thing?"

"Yep," said Soraiya. "There'll be another submarine on the other side of that dividing wall." She glanced at her watch. "We need to hurry, you guys. Okay. You two will be over here, Mario and I will be over there. We'll position our sub someplace where we think you won't be able to find it. You'll do the same. Then we'll take turns calling shots." She pointed to the bottom of the pool, which was marked off in a ten-by-ten grid. One side was marked with the letters, the other with numbers. "You know, A-one, C-nine, stuff like that."

"Actually," said Haley, hoisting a wobbly water balloon out of a battleship-gray crate, "I think we're just supposed to toss these over the wall at each other."

"Cool," said Simon. "That sounds way more fun."

Suddenly, turbulent waves started churning across the water, rocking the submarine. A siren *A-OOGA*ed.

"Battle stations," announced a stern voice in the ceiling. "Battle stations!"

"This is going to be so awesome!" said Soraiya. "Come on, Mario!"

They hurried to the far side of the wall, grabbed a double armload of water balloons, and climbed into the two open hatches on top of their bobbing submarine.

"Let's drive it over there," whispered Soraiya.

"Good move," Simon whispered back. "I think Carolyn is buying my Mario act."

"Totally," said Soraiya.

"Um, I've never been in a boat before."

"Don't worry! I have. Found the gas pedal!"

And the small boat bounded across the surging surf.

"Do you get seasick?" asked Soraiya as the tiny sub cut across the waves.

"I hope not," said Simon.

"Me too," said Soraiya. "Because I'm sitting in front of you. Okay. We'll park here." She piloted the submarine to a spot very close to the dividing wall.

"Oooh," whispered Simon. "Clever move."

"You guys ready over there?" Soraiya cried out.

"Totally!" shouted Carolyn. "You guys toss your balloon first!"

Simon lobbed a wobbly water balloon up and over the wall.

Two seconds later, there was a splash.

"Miss!" shouted Haley and Carolyn.

"Our turn!" said Carolyn. "Here it comes!"

Simon looked up.

And saw a blubbery blue balloon wobbling through the air. It was coming down straight at him.

Before he could duck or cover his head, the balloon smacked him right in the face and exploded.

He was drenched.

His shirt was soaked.

"Direct hit," he said with a laugh, swiping away some of the water.

Soraiya gasped.

And it didn't take Simon long to figure out why.

Going cross-eyed, he looked down and saw his rubber nose dangling off the tip of his real one.

His fake chin?

Stuck to his shirt.

"How'd we do?" hollered Haley.

"You got us good," said Soraiya as she tried to help Simon reattach his rubbery disguise.

Simon heard footsteps on the other side of the wall. Someone ran into the room.

"You two done? We got next."

It was Jack McClintock. He was out of breath.

"It's all yours," said Haley.

Simon heard Haley and Carolyn climb out of their sub and exit the exhibit.

"I need glue!" he whispered to Soraiya.

"You need to fix your wig, too. Hurry!"

More footsteps.

It sounded like Jack and Andrew were coming around to Soraiya and Simon's side of the pool.

"So," said Jack, "you guys should probably switch sides for this next match like they do in volley—"

He did not finish that thought.

He was too busy staring at Simon, who was sitting in the submarine holding his nose, his chin, and his hair in his hands.

"Excuse me, sir," said Mr. Raymo, tapping Mr. Lemoncello on the shoulder. "I hate to interrupt your enjoyment of the jug band's clog dancing routine, but Jack McClintock is in the atrium, yelling at your interactive oil painting."

"Oh, dear. Is there some problem?"

"Apparently."

"It might be best if you had a word with him," coached Dr. Zinchenko.

"Very well," said Mr. Lemoncello. "Bring me the portable portrait-cam!"

Mr. Raymo rolled a black cube with a pair of velvet curtains at one end over to Mr. Lemoncello. Video cables dangled out of the opposite side. Mr. Lemoncello pulled back the curtains and stuck his head inside the box, which was equipped with a holographic camera linked to the talking portrait in the museum's atrium. There was also a miniature monitor so Mr. Lemoncello could see who was talking to him.

"Halloooo!" he shouted into the camera lens. "How may I be of assistance, Jack?"

Inside the atrium, all the contestants had gathered under the jumbo-sized portrait of Mr. Lemoncello.

"What seems to be the problem?" asked the holographic painting.

"This cheater isn't Mario the supergamer from Ohio!" screamed Jack. "He's a local joker named Simon Skrindle!"

"Whoa, ease up, rude dude," said Akimi.

"What's Simon Skrindle doing here?" Jack demanded.

"He's playing with me," said Soraiya.

"Kyle Keeley is sick," Haley tried to explain. "We needed someone to take his place."

"So we gave him a slight disguise," said Akimi.

Jack turned on Andrew. "Did you know about this?"

"Yes," said Andrew proudly. "I did."

"This is so illegal!" shouted Jack. He wanted Simon out of the game. Mostly because he knew, better than anyone in Hudson Hills, what a skilled gamer the guy actually was. If Jack could get Simon ejected, he'd eliminate his number one threat.

"Look," Jack said to the Lemoncello portrait, "the rules of this game were pretty clear. Each winner of the sidewalk board game would be teamed up with one of the gamers from Ohio. Simon Skrindle doesn't live in Ohio. Therefore, Soraiya is disqualified. She needs to leave here, now."

"Not so fast, Jack," boomed Mr. Lemoncello. "You are, of course, correct. Those *were* the official rules when the game began. But, Mario—I mean, Simon—tell me: Did you at any point during your game play today pick up, oh, let's say a bonus card?"

Simon nodded. "Yes, sir. We did pretty well on the Connect Four game and—"

"No you did not!" said Jack. "What a liar. Andrew and I beat those two."

"It's true, sir," said Andrew, looking up at the painting. "We did."

"But then we had to play a second game," said Soraiya. "Simon gave four answers when we only needed to give one!"

"And for that," declared Mr. Lemoncello, "he was presented with a bonus card made out of rubber, is that correct, Simon?"

"Yes, sir." He held up the wobbly rubber card.

"Ah, yes!" said Mr. Lemoncello. "That's a bendable bonus card if ever I've seen one, and I've seen a billion, right next door at the factory on rubber-molding day! That card, Simon, is good for bending one rule. Would you like to cash it in?"

"Yes, sir," said Simon. "I would."

"Very good. And which rule would you like to bend?"

"Um, the one about partners having to be from Ohio. I want to finish the game with Soraiya!"

"That's what I want, too!" said Soraiya.

"Very well, Soraiya. But I am duty-bound to inform you: Should you win, you will have to *share* your titanium ticket and your slot in the tournament finals with Simon Skrindle, since he is also a resident of Hudson Hills. Do you find these terms acceptable?"

"Yes, sir. I do."

Simon felt adrenaline rush through his body. He had a chance to win a titanium ticket and take over Mr. Lemoncello's whole game-making empire with Soraiya? That would be so much fun. She could be the big cheese. He'd dream up all the games. What had been the worst day of his life might turn into the best!

"Very well," announced Mr. Lemoncello, "that rule has been bent, but like a stout-hearted willow tree in a stiff breeze, it is not broken. Play on, contestants! Play on!"

"B-b-but . . . ," Jack sputtered.

"Jack?" said Mr. Lemoncello. "You're sputtering when you should be playing. The clock is ticking. The sand is shifting. It's seven-ten. It's time to start gaming again!"

"You let him spend the day at the company picnic?" huffed Simon's grandfather as he hiked up the factory hill with Simon's grandmother.

"Take it easy, Sam," said his grandmother. "It's no big deal. I just wanted Simon to get out of the house and have a little fun."

"We should've discussed it first, Sophia!"

"Why? You would've just said no. Honestly, Samuel, you have to let go of your anger. Making life miserable for Simon won't bring Stephen back!"

"I will not have my grandson destroyed by that evil man."

"Mr. Lemoncello isn't evil. He brings joy to children all over the world."

"Joy? He killed our son, Sophia. Killed our daughter-in-law, too. Mr. Lemoncello made Simon an orphan!"

"No, he didn't. It was an accident. . . ."

"Which only happened because of Luigi L. Lemoncello!"

They reached the factory and saw a crowd in the parking lot enjoying a jug band performance. At the edge of the mob, Simon's grandfather could see a man dressed in a security guard uniform.

"The guard might know where Simon is," he muttered. "Excuse me, sir."

"Hang on, old-timer," said the security guard, whose shirt identified him as Buck McClintock. "Mr. Lemoncello has his head stuck in a box. I think he's talking to the kids inside the building. Something big must be going on. . . ."

"We're looking for our grandson." Simon's grandfather showed Mr. McClintock Simon's seventh-grade class picture. "His name is Simon Skrindle."

The security guard peered at him. "So that makes you Sam Skrindle, right? The guy who writes all those loony letters to the editor about Mr. Lemoncello?"

"They are not 'loony,' sir. They are true."

"Not completely, dear," said Simon's grandmother.

"Hang on, Pops," said McClintock. "It looks like Mr. Lemoncello is going to make some kind of announcement. . . ."

"I don't care about—"

"Shh!"

Mr. Lemoncello stepped up to the microphone on the bandstand.

"Ladies and gentlemen, boys and girls, hamsters and gerbils. I am pleased to report that there are now *five* sons and daughters of Gameworks employees vying for the first titanium ticket: Carolyn Hudson, Piya Sarkarati, Soraiya Mitchell, Jack McClintock, and Simon Skrindle, the player formerly known as Mario."

"What?" shouted Mr. McClintock. "What happened to Mario?"

"Surprise!" said Mr. Lemoncello. "He was really Simon all along."

"That's cheating! The kid snuck in!"

"No, Mr. McClintock. It is not cheating or even Cheetos. Because earlier today, Simon, previously known as Mario, and his partner, Soraiya, earned a bendable bonus card."

"Oh, those are good!" shouted a man in the crowd.

"With one of those, you can bend any rule in the book," added a woman.

"And," said another factory worker, "they're made out of high-quality, very durable styrene-butadiene rubber!"

"Indeed they are!" cried Mr. Lemoncello. "So nobody has to sing 'Oops, there goes another rubber tree plant.' Soraiya and Simon chose to bend the rule about coaches coming exclusively from Ohio. Since both Simon and Soraiya live right here in Hudson Hills, they will now both be eligible to move on to the Bazillion-Dollar Final Round, should they be the contestants who first solve all the puzzles, fill in all the bubbles, and find the titanium ticket hidden inside the Board Game Hall of Fame."

"That's my girl!" shouted Mr. Mitchell, doing a double arm pump.

"That's my grandson," seethed Simon's grandfather.

"Simon Skrindle shouldn't be in there," muttered Mr. McClintock.

"Agreed," said Simon's grandfather.

"Samuel?" pleaded his grandmother. "Please. Let the boy have his fun. It's only a game."

"Life isn't a game, Sophia." Simon's grandfather ignored his wife and gestured at the giant ring of keys clipped to Mr. McClintock's belt. "Any of those get us into this hall of fame that Lemoncello's yakking about?"

"All of them," the security guard replied, hoisting up his pants.

"And I suppose you wouldn't mind your boy, Jack, having one less competitor in there, eh?"

Mr. McClintock smiled. "You're a very wise man, Mr. Skrindle. We should probably use a back door."

"Yes," said Simon's grandfather. "The one with the fewest security cameras."

"Nobody's watching those security cameras, except me. And, right now, I have a new assignment: escorting you into the building to talk some sense into your grandson. He needs to quit."

"Trust me," said Mr. Skrindle. "Once I tell Simon what Mr. Lemoncello did to his father and mother, he will."

"Samuel?" Simon's grandmother tried once more. "Don't do this. Please."

He ignored her.

"Take me inside, Mr. McClintock. It's time Simon knew the truth."

"Um, was anybody here when the clock struck seven?" Simon asked the group in the atrium.

Jack glared at him.

"No," he sneered. "We were upstairs at the Battleship exhibit, watching you lose your wig and nose, remember?"

"Riiight . . ."

"Come on, Andrew. I need to clobber you with a water balloon."

"B-b-but . . . ," Andrew protested.

"Upstairs," said Jack. "The iPad says I can play Battleship against anybody, and I sure don't want to play it against any of these cheaters. They'd probably all bend another rule."

"Actually," Andrew tried to explain, "a bendable card can only be used one time per—"

"Shut up, Andy. We need to be upstairs."

Jack stomped up the staircase. It played a very sour tune. Andrew hurried along after him.

"Come on, Piya," said Akimi. "Let's go finish our railroad."

Piya sighed. "It's taking so long. Thank goodness it counts as two games and we'll get extra letters!"

They went over to the elevator bank to ride up to the fourth floor.

"We were here at seven," said Carolyn. "It was amazing!" She pointed to the frozen figurines lined up behind the clock's upper glass door.

"You see those kids? They're all playing games. They twirl and spin and dance. . . ."

"It was pretty cool," added Haley. "There's a little Luigi Lemoncello with a hinged jaw. Every hour, he tosses back his head and laughs because all the other carved characters around him are having so much fun."

"And when he laughed," said Carolyn, "the moon phase dial started to glow with an image of the man in the moon. He was laughing, too!"

"I want to be here at eight to see it," said Simon.

"No problem," said Soraiya. "But first we need to win the game."

"That's not going to happen, young lady," said a stern voice. A stooped man stepped out of a shadowy hallway and into the atrium. "At least not with Simon."

"Grandpa?" said Simon.

"We need to talk," he said. "In private."

"Simon?" said Soraiya, as the grandfather clock chimed its four-note melody. "We're running out of time. It's seven-fifteen! We only have until eight. That's the deadline. There's a chance nobody will win the titanium ticket."

"This will only take a minute," said Simon's grandfather. "There's a room over here, Simon. It's empty."

"Soooo, Carolyn," said Haley, "how about we go to the snack bar and eat another one of those lemon-cream-filled chocolate cellos we found earlier?"

"Good idea."

Carolyn and Haley scurried out of the atrium and headed for the snack bar.

"I'm sorry, Grandpa," said Simon, "but if you're going to yell at me for going to the company picnic and playing games and having fun—"

"I'm not gonna yell at you, Simon. I'm simply going to tell you something I should've told you years ago."

Simon's grandfather turned around and strode through a door to enter a gloomy side room. Most of the Board Game Hall of Fame was lit up like a video arcade or amusement park. It figured that Simon's grim grandfather would pick the dreariest room in the building for their chat.

"I'll be back," Simon said to Soraiya.

She nodded.

And Simon followed his grandfather into the darkened chamber.

It was a stark room with a high ceiling—maybe twenty feet tall.

There was a wide, museum-style stone bench in the center of the space, illuminated by one dim light overhead.

"Simon, I'll be brief," said his grandfather, his voice ringing off the walls, which might've been made of marble (Simon couldn't see them). "We never told you much when you asked what happened to your father and mother."

"I know it was a 'tragic accident in Asia.' "

Simon's grandfather nodded. "Your father and mother both worked for Mr. Lemoncello. They were his top employees. He sent them off to China, together. Said he needed the two of them to scout out a new location for his Gameworks Factory. Their flight home went down over the Pacific. Your mother and father both died. Long story short: Mr. Lemoncello killed them. So, Simon, you think long and hard about what you're doing here. But if I were you, I sure wouldn't want anything to do with the man who murdered my parents and made me an orphan."

With that, Simon's grandfather turned and walked away.

Simon sat down on the stone bench and heard someone heave a heavy sigh.

"Well, I guess that's one way to tell the story," said a soft voice that seemed to be coming from the ceiling.

It was Mr. Lemoncello, but not like Simon had ever heard him before. He sounded sad.

"I hope you'll forgive me, Simon, but, well, I couldn't help but eavesdrop on your conversation with your grandfather. What he told you isn't completely true. I loved your father and mother. Why, if it weren't for them, this factory would have remained but a twinkle in my eye. They took my wacky ideas and turned them into something real. Your father was my head engineer. Your mother was in charge of quality control."

Soft lights started to slowly brighten the darkened room.

“Your parents met right here at the factory. I was the best man at their wedding. Not that I’m bragging . . .”

As the lights came up, Simon realized that the room’s twenty-foot-tall walls *were* marble, just like he thought they might be. It felt like he was visiting the Lincoln Memorial or some other landmark down in Washington, D.C.

“I suppose I should have insisted that they fly on different planes whenever they traveled for business. Especially after you came along. But those two lovebirds were inseparable.”

Now the lights in the room fell on a sleek marble wall with words chiseled into the stone:

THE FUTURE BELONGS TO THE PUZZLE SOLVERS.
THIS BUILDING IS DEDICATED
TO ALL THE CLEVER ENGINEERS
WHO HAVE MADE SO MANY
WILD AND FANTASTICAL IDEAS LEAP TO LIFE.
MOST ESPECIALLY SALLY AND STEPHEN SKRINDLE.

Simon studied the words. He read them, over and over.

Mr. Lemoncello remained silent until, finally, he spoke.

“This entire Board Game Hall of Fame was built as a tribute to your parents, Simon.”

“Is this why you wanted me to be one of the first to see everything inside here?” Simon asked. “To see this?”

“Yes, Simon.”

"Thank you, sir."

It felt odd, talking to the vast emptiness of the marble room, having a conversation with someone who wasn't actually there. Odd and strangely soothing.

"How did my parents die?" Simon asked, his voice breaking.

"In a plane crash. Just like your grandfather said. They had indeed flown to China, looking for a new location for my Gameworks Factory. Somewhere with cheaper labor costs. But your parents convinced me that cheaper doesn't always mean better. That was our last phone call. And, Simon?"

"Yes, sir?"

"Because of your father and mother and their final request, I will never ever even think about moving my factory out of Hudson Hills."

Now Mr. Lemoncello sounded like *he* might be choking up.

"I wish I had known them as well as you did, sir."

"Me too, Simon. Me too. By the way—I've noted how clever and resourceful you are. It's another reason you were meant to be here this evening. When I watch you, I am reminded of them."

"Really?"

"Really. Now then, I will completely understand if you no longer wish to participate in this evening's quest. In life, as in board games, we are all responsible for the path we decide to follow." Mr. Lemoncello was starting to sound like his old self. "The choice is yours. This voice is mine. Toodle-oo, Simon. I'm glad we could have this man-to-man, ceiling-to-bench talk!"

"Me too."

Simon sat quietly for a moment, staring at the memorial wall.

"You okay?"

Soraiya stepped into the room. She looked at the impressive marble wall.

"Wow. Stephen and Sally Skrindle. They're your parents, right?"

Simon nodded. "Mr. Lemoncello dedicated this whole place to my father and mother."

"So what do you want to do now, Simon?" asked Soraiya. "Pass or play?"

Simon thought about that. He could just go home and spend the rest of the night sulking up in the attic.

But is that what his mom and dad would've done?

He smiled. He was all done with holding himself back and getting in his own way.

"Well, Soraiya, like the wall says, 'The future belongs to the puzzle solvers.' Let's go solve some more puzzles, fast. We need to win this thing!"

"We have four more exhibits to go," said Soraiya as they jogged back into the atrium. "But we only have forty minutes to finish. We can budget ten minutes per exhibit. . . ."

"Where to next?"

"The third floor. We should take this ladder."

"Why not the elevator?"

"Because this ladder wasn't here earlier. It's a new piece for the game."

Simon studied the ladder. It extended down into a trapdoor. Looking up, he saw that it angled into a glass wall on the third floor.

"The lPad wants us to play Chutes and Ladders next," said Soraiya. "In the game, chutes are bad. They make you drop back several spaces. Ladders, on the other hand, are good. They help you skip spaces. And right now"—she nodded toward the ticking grandfather clock—"we need to skip as many spaces as we can!"

She stepped onto the ladder. When both her feet were steady, metal safety clamps popped up to lock her shoes in place.

"Safety first," she said with a laugh. "It's the plant manager's motto!"

Suddenly, the ladder's rungs started moving. The tread Soraiya was standing on hauled her skyward. The ladder had turned into an escalator.

"Jump on!" she shouted to Simon.

"What? Are you nuts?"

"The safety clamps will stop you from falling off. Hurry!"

Simon thought about what happened the last time he tried to scale something. He had ended up on his butt in the burbling crater of a chocolate volcano.

"It's fun, Simon!" cried Soraiya as she glided upward. "Just climb aboard. It's what Mario would do."

"I am Mario!" hollered Simon as he leapt onto the moving ladder. Safety clamps grabbed his sneakers and held them tight.

The escalator ladder carried Soraiya and Simon higher and higher on a slight slant. Simon dared a look over his shoulder as he passed the grandfather clock.

"So cool!"

He had an excellent view of the figurines ready to spring into action behind the clock's glass door.

Soon they were twenty feet off the floor.

Then thirty.

Then forty.

Then Simon closed his eyes and refused to look down.

When he passed through the wall on the third floor and the clamps securing his feet sprang free, Simon hopped off the ladder and hurried over to where Soraiya was already studying a 3-D rebus puzzle projected in front of the blank black wall.

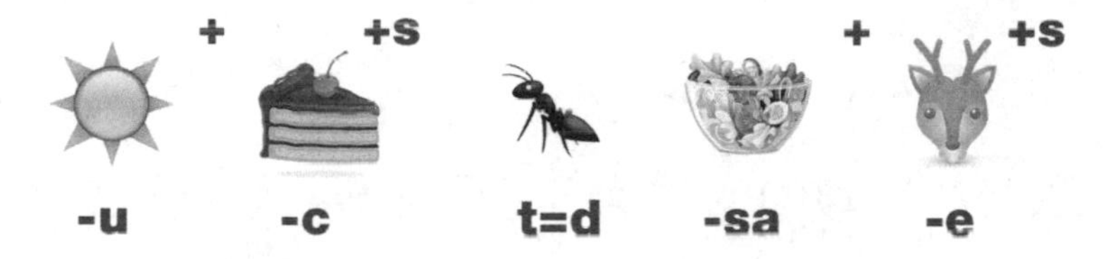

"Okay," she said, "suncakes plus moose salad equals indigestion?"

"Actually, you're supposed to take the 'U' out of 'sun,' leaving 'S-N,' then you—"

"Simon?"

"Yeah?"

"We're kind of in a hurry, remember? Just solve it."

"Okay. 'Snakes and Ladders.' "

"Of course," said Soraiya. "That was the original name for the game we now call Chutes and Ladders. My dad taught me that."

The lPad made a sparkly *GLING* sound.

"Whoa," said Soraiya. "It's also the answer to our fifth

word puzzle. Six letters, three letters, seven letters. Snakes and Ladders!"

She quickly tapped in the string of three words.

SNAKES AND LADDERS

6 11 24 32 47 2 17

The screen dissolved and the numbered letters took their places in the seventy-six-letter phrase.

"This is starting to make sense!" Soraiya remarked when she read the revised screen:

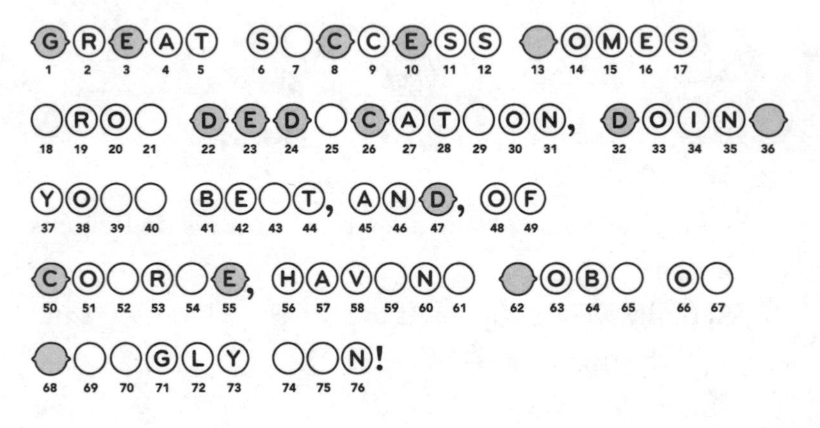

Simon peered over her shoulder and tried deciphering the phrase: "Great success comes from dedication, doing your best, and, of course, uh, having . . . something . . ."

"An oboe?" said Soraiya.

"No. It's blank, 'O-B,' blank . . ."

Suddenly, the lPad screen changed from the phrase to a spinner with a red arrow and a circle cut into six colored slices, each one with a number.

“Huh,” said Soraiya. “That’s different.”

“Flick it,” suggested Simon.

Soraiya tapped the image of the pointer. It twirled and spun and landed on the blue five.

Five illuminated four-by-four-foot squares appeared on the floor. Blue, white, blue, white, blue.

“I think we’re supposed to advance to the fifth space, the blue one,” said Soraiya. “Like in a board game.”

“Together?” asked Simon.

Soraiya shrugged. “Guess so. We’re a team.”

They held hands and hopped their way to the fifth square.

When they landed on it, Simon heard something click.

The floor didn’t feel so firm.

Then it fell away.

Simon and Soraiya dropped down into a very long and windy chute! Simon’s stomach felt as if it had just lurched up to somewhere behind his nose.

“Hang on,” cried Soraiya. “It’s a waterslide without any water! Woo-hoo!”

Simon wasn't enjoying the slide down the winding gerbil tube as much as Soraiya seemed to be.

They were falling so fast his cheeks were fluttering as they whipped through a corkscrew of twists and turns.

"At least it's not a straight drop!" shouted Soraiya.

That's when they dropped about ten feet straight down into another series of wicked switchbacks.

So that's why I saw those clear tubes snaking through the atrium, Simon thought. They were the "snakes" from Snakes and Ladders. The chutes from the more modern version of the game.

"Close your eyes!" cried Soraiya as they flew through the hard plastic tube. "Here comes the floor."

Simon dared to look down.

The floor was coming up at them fast.

The Board Game Hall of Fame wasn't officially open to the public. They were the first ones riding this ride! What if it didn't work? What if they crash-landed?

Suddenly, there was a *FWOMP* and a *SWOOSH*.

A circular chunk of stone the size of a manhole cover flopped down. A burst of lemon-scented compressed air shot up from the basement and buffeted Simon and Soraiya, making their baggy, sweaty clothes balloon up into thick cotton parachutes.

"We're slowing down!" said Soraiya. "It's like we're inside a pneumatic tube."

They slowly drifted down, eased through the hole in the floor, dropped out of the bottom of the chute, and plopped into a barrel filled with foam rubber fruit.

"Now that we're still alive," said Soraiya, who, like Simon, was sprawled on her back in a bed of squishy fruit-shaped balls, "I have to admit: That was awesome."

"Yeah," Simon agreed. "It was."

They both grabbed hold of the lip of the barrel and pulled themselves up to survey their surroundings.

"That barrel over there is filled with apples," said Simon. "Wonder why it's down in the basement."

"Could be a future Apples to Apples exhibit," said Soraiya.

"Is that another game?" asked Simon.

"Yep." Soraiya hauled herself out of the barrel. Simon was right behind her.

"Huh," said Simon, reading what was written on the barrel they'd landed in. "These ones aren't apples. They're figs."

"Well, that's weird. I don't think there's a game called Figs to Figs. . . ."

The lPad *BA-BLING*ed again.

"New riddle," said Soraiya, staring at the screen. " 'What did the three little figs say to the big bad wolf when he told them to open their doors?' "

"You mean the three little *pigs*. . . ."

"Nope. It's the three little figs. Hang on. They're giving us the first words. We need to fill in the last three. . . ."

NOT BY THE HAIR OF OUR

○○○○○ ○○○ ○○○○

18 25 36 61 67 29 62 74 59 70 65

"My grandmother used to read 'The Three Little Pigs' to me when I was little," said Simon. "The pigs say, 'Not by the hair of our chinny-chin-chins.' But there aren't enough bubbles for that."

"So," reasoned Soraiya, "counting the letters and applying Lemoncello logic, the three figs might say, 'Not by the hair of our figgy-fig-figs.' "

Soraiya tapped in the answer. The lPad trumpeted a tinny fanfare and the numbered letters flew to their appropriate spots.

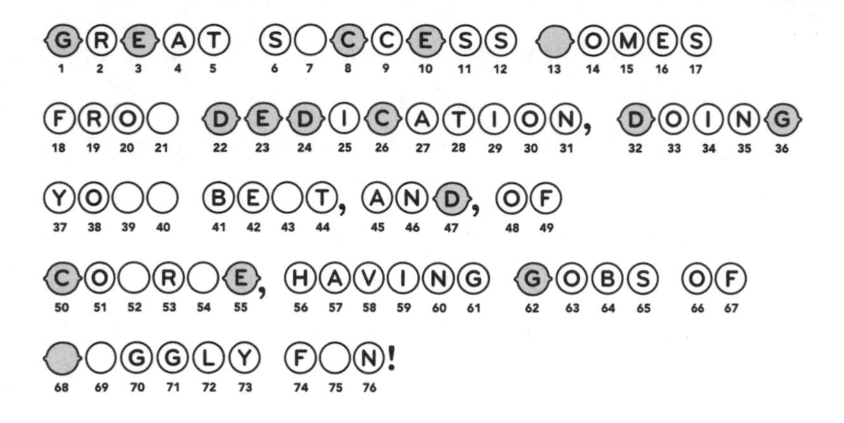

"I think I can solve it now!" said Simon. "Great success comes from dedication, doing your best, and, of course, having gobs of giggly fun!"

"You might be right," said Soraiya. "But we have thirty-five minutes and only two more exhibits to visit. We shouldn't jump to conclusions."

"But I really think we can assume we know what those letters are."

"Scientists never assume, Simon. It's against all the rules of the scientific method. And those, my friend, cannot be bent, even if you have a rubbery bonus card!"

Simon nodded. "So where to next?"

Soraiya studied the lPad. "Big-Time Boggle. Second floor."

When she finished saying that, a new escalator ladder rose up out of the basement floor and headed for the ceiling, which was actually the atrium floor, where a trapdoor slid open.

“Looks like that ladder is headed to where we need to go,” said Simon.

This time, he climbed aboard first. Soraiya hopped on right after him.

“Let’s just hope that every ladder doesn’t come with a chute,” she remarked. “Because the second chute may not have such a soft and figgy landing!”

Meanwhile, on the fourth floor, Akimi and Piya were about to complete their sixth game.

After they'd finally finished their Ticket to Ride transcontinental railroad (and earned two sets of letter-filled bubbles instead of just one), they had ridden that railroad across a towering trestle bridge to the mysterious island of Catan, a strange land made up of interlocking hexagons.

Now they were settlers, looking for bricks, lumber, wool, grain, and ore to build a city.

"Do you think Mr. Lemoncello knows that my dream is to become a civil engineer?" asked Piya as she and Akimi chased after an audio-animatronic sheep (at least Akimi hoped it was audio-animatronic) in their quest for wool. "Is that why our path through the hall of fame has included so many building games?"

"Maybe," said Akimi, right before she dove for the

ankles of the mechanical sheep—and missed. She landed in a very realistic-smelling pile of artificial sheep dung.

On the second floor, Haley and Carolyn were playing a game called Encore, where they had to come up with songs containing a certain word, such as "lemon."

This was their second-to-last game, but Carolyn wasn't in a hurry.

She just wanted Haley to hear how well she sang!

Also on the second floor, Simon and Soraiya found the Big-Time Boggle display. It was an eight-foot see-through plastic cube with sixteen letter blocks arrayed on a four-by-four tray in its floor. When you looked through the plastic dome, only the top letter of each block was visible.

"We have to shake up the letters and then make sixteen four-letter words out of the sixteen letters facing up after our shake," said Soraiya, reading the instructions off her lPad. "So, it's just like Boggle. Only bigger."

"But how do we shake up the letters?" wondered Simon. "The box is huge."

"We have to push the shake button."

"Great. Where is it?"

Simon and Soraiya examined the exterior of the eight-foot cube. They couldn't find a button.

Until one started glowing.

Inside the cube.

"I'll do it," said Simon, lifting a hinged panel on the clear cube's side. "Huh. The walls are cushioned. Like the plastic's puffed up with air or something."

He climbed into the letter box.

"Hang on," said Soraiya. "We're a team. We'll do it together."

She ducked down, stepped in, and walked across the soft and squishy letter cubes to join Simon near the button.

"Ready?" said Simon.

Soraiya nodded. "On your mark, get set, lemon, cello, go!"

Simon pressed the button. The eight-foot cube bucked up and down. Hydraulic pistons in the floor rocked it and rolled it, shaking it like a paint-mixing machine at the hardware store. Letters started tumbling. So did Simon and Soraiya.

"H-h-how l-l-long w-w-will th-th-this th-th-thing sh-sh-shake?" Simon shouted as he and Soraiya bobbled and bounced.

"I—I—I h-h-have n-n-no i-i-idea!" Soraiya shouted back. Then she and Simon bounced around some more.

"That's hysterical!" said Jack, laughing.

He was watching Simon and Soraiya being shaken inside the Boggle box on his phone. He could also see Haley and Carolyn singing while Akimi and Piya pushed a wheelbarrow full of iron ore. The screen of his phone was divided into a grid of images, each one corresponding to one of the security cameras inside the Board Game Hall of Fame.

The CCTV app was a perk of being the head of security's son. It was excellent for tracking his opponents' progress. He tucked his phone back into the side pocket of his camo cargo pants so his partner, Peckleman, couldn't see him using it.

They'd just completed the seventh game. Which was why Andrew was off in a corner, trying to wipe the yellow sludge off his glasses. Their seventh game had been played with Pimple Pete, a ten-foot-tall replica of the goo-shooting plastic head from the grossest board game ever invented (so far). The thing moved around on hidden wheels like a ginormous remote-controlled car.

"Well," said Andrew, rubbing another glob of fake pimple gunk off his shirt, "that was definitely explosive fun for the whole family."

"Hey," said Jack, "check this out." He'd moved around behind Pimple Pete's giant plastic head. "There's a controller tucked into a nook back here. You can manually override the big head's preprogrammed moves. You can make Pimple Pete do whatever you want him to do."

"There's also a label on the controller that says 'For staff use only,' " remarked Andrew.

"I'm on the staff," said Jack, prying the remote out of its cubbyhole.

"No you're not."

"I help my dad all the time," Jack insisted. He removed

the remote and fiddled with its color-coded buttons. They were set up like the ones on an Xbox controller for PlayStation. The huge head moved forward, backward, sideways. Its pulsing pimples blinked. Its red nose bulged and glowed.

"Where do we go next?" Jack asked Andrew as he continued fiddling with the controller, making Pimple Pete spin in circles.

"Um, Pimple Pete's puzzle gave us every letter we needed except two," said Andrew, checking the screen on their IPad. "And those last two are lemons. . . ."

"What's our eighth and final game?"

"Guess Who? The mystery face game from Milton Bradley," said Andrew. "The exhibit for it is on the first floor."

"Great. And guess who I'm taking with us?" Jack thumbed the remote. Pimple Pete whirred forward.

"No. You. Are. Not," said Andrew.

"Look, Andy. Soraiya and Simon are on their seventh game, too. There's only like thirty minutes left. If they come gunning for us, we can slime them with Pimple Pete. Slow 'em down."

Andrew bristled. "That would be cheating!"

"No. I'm just angling for a tactical advantage."

"That's it. You are *not* going to pull a Chiltington on me! You, sir, are on your own! I quit."

"Fine. I don't need you. And if that idiot Simon Skrindle can bend the rules, so can I!"

Simon and Soraiya stepped out of the tumbling Boggle box, feeling the way socks probably feel when they come out of the dryer.

"You okay?" Simon asked.

"Yeah," replied Soraiya. "I'm just glad we never had time to eat one of those ham and cheese ice cream sandwiches."

The lPad made a *ZZZZZIIIP* sound.

Sixteen letters—four rows of four letters each—matching the sixteen now in the grid on the floor of the Big-Time Boggle box filled the screen:

U B R H
U L U M
I Q M T
U S S P

"Okay," said Soraiya, after reading the game's instructions, "this is a little different from regular Boggle. We now have three minutes to find at least sixteen four-letter words using these sixteen letters."

A green light inside the clear cube started blinking.

"Blip," said Simon. "Bump!"

"Burp," added Soraiya. "Hips, hubs, hums . . ."

Simon took over. "Limb, limp, mist, er . . . mush!"

The green light changed to yellow.

"We only have two minutes left," said Soraiya.

Simon rubbed his stubbly hair. The pressure was on. He didn't want to let Soraiya down. And what about Jack? Had he and Andrew already figured out the seventy-six-letter phrase? He started humming.

"Why are you humming? We already did 'hums.' "

"Music helps me think," said Simon. He put himself up in his attic with his glockenspiel. He saw the notes. Saw the colors. Then, in a flash, he saw words that Soraiya and he hadn't seen before.

"Plum, push, rump, slip . . ."

"Spur!" shouted Soraiya.

The light turned red. They had one minute.

"Pits!" cried Simon.

The lPad sounded another tinny fanfare.

"You did it!" shouted Soraiya.

"No," said Simon, "*we* did it."

He leaned in to look at the tablet.

"There's no riddle? Just sixteen letter bubbles? What

sixteen-letter word are we looking for? How many letters does 'Lemoncello' have in it?"

"Ten."

"How about 'Luigi Lemoncello'?"

"Fifteen," said Soraiya. "But the rules never said the answer to every game had to be an actual word or words. . . ."

"What are you thinking?"

"We've just been staring at sixteen letters! I'll try those!"

"Good idea! See what happens."

Soraiya typed the sixteen letters into the sixteen bubbles.

U B R H U L U M I Q M T U S S P
7 40 52 75 69 21 39 43 54

The tablet *GLING*ed to let them know they were correct.

"Whoa!" said Soraiya. "Check it out!"

As the screen dissolved from the sixteen-letter answer to the seventy-six-letter phrase, only two letters remained blank: the lemons at 13 and 68.

G R E A T S U C C E S S _ O M E S
1 2 3 4 5 6 7 8 9 10 11 12 13 14 15 16 17

F R O M D E D I C A T I O N, D O I N G
18 19 20 21 22 23 24 25 26 27 28 29 30 31 32 33 34 35 36

Y O U R B E S T, A N D, O F
37 38 39 40 41 42 43 44 45 46 47 48 49

C O U R S E, H A V I N G G O B S O F
50 51 52 53 54 55 56 57 58 59 60 61 62 63 64 65 66 67

_ I G G L Y F U N!
68 69 70 71 72 73 74 75 76

"The last two lemony letters have to be 'C' and 'G'!" said Simon. "That last bit has to be 'gobs of giggly fun.' "

"What if your hypothesis is incorrect?" countered Soraiya. "What if it's gobs of wiggly or jiggly fun? What if we guess incorrectly instead of gathering the final two pieces of data? According to my watch, we still have sixteen minutes."

"Okay, okay. We do this the right way. We play on."

"One more game and we're done, Simon! Guess Who?"

"Um, you're Soraiya."

"Correct. That's also the name of our last game. Guess Who? It's on this floor. Near the far wall to the west."

They took off running.

Simon could hear the clock down in the atrium doing its *bing-bong-bing-bong* thing three times in a row. That meant it was 7:45.

"Now we only have fifteen minutes!" cried Soraiya.

"No problem," said Simon. "We only have one game left. We can win this thing."

They hurried under the arched entrance into the Guess Who? exhibit.

Mounted on the far wall were twenty-four flat-panel video monitors, arranged in three rows of eight. Each one of the screens had a slightly animated cartoon face displayed on it. The twenty-four faces blinked. And smiled. One labeled "Sam" fidgeted with his glasses.

Suddenly, all twenty-four panels started flashing.

"Your character is now being selected," boomed a game-show-sounding announcer. "Guess who!"

The TVs returned to their portrait modes. The cartoons kept smiling.

"We have to figure out which of the twenty-four faces the computer just selected before time runs out," Soraiya whispered to Simon. "We can ask questions to narrow down the field."

A two-minute digital clock started counting down.

"Go for it," said Simon.

"Is our person a female?" asked Soraiya.

"Yes," said the game show announcer.

Nineteen of the twenty-four faces, all of the males, faded to black.

"Seriously?" said Soraiya. "There are only five female figures in this whole game? What's up with that?"

"Guess it's an antique," said Simon. "Must be why it's in a museum."

Soraiya was about to ask her second question when Jack McClintock burst into the room.

And he wasn't alone.

"Stop the game!" Jack shouted as he thumbed the buttons on a small controller he clutched.

A giant plastic head with a queasy expression on its face lumbered into the room. The white bumps dotting its chin, cheeks, and forehead throbbed as if they were ready to burst. So did the bright-red beacon on its nose.

"You guys remember Pimple Pete," said Jack. "Looks like his nose is about to blow."

"This is so gross," Soraiya muttered.

She and Simon reflexively took one step backward as the big pimple-popping head swerved on its wobbly wheels.

"You two don't mind if I play through, do you?" Jack said. "This is my last game. Then I win."

"Actually," said Simon, "we were here first."

"And we've already started our game," said Soraiya.

"You're smart, Soraiya Mitchell," said Jack. "You fooled everybody. Except me."

"Huh?"

"Everybody thinks you teamed up with Simon—even disguised him as Mario—because you felt sorry for him. But you know what I know. Simon Skrindle is good at these Lemoncello games. He's an idiot about everything else. But games? Oh, he's a sneaky little genius."

"I'm also pretty good at music," Simon mumbled.

"Shut up!" snarled Jack. He jabbed the blue button on his controller. The giant plastic head lurched forward.

Startled, Simon and Soraiya jumped back.

The floor panel they landed on flopped open.

They fell down another hole.

Soraiya had been right.

For every ladder, there had to be another chute.

They flew through the swirly tube down to the atrium.

Compressed air shot up again, buffeting their descent, slowing them down.

They made another soft landing, this time in the Apples to Apples barrel.

"We need to be back up on the second floor!" said Soraiya, standing up in the squeaky-ball apple pit. She had to shout to be heard over the massive fan still blowing compressed air up the empty tube.

"Hang on," said Simon. "I think I know a shortcut."

"What?"

"We can ride one of these apples like it's a Ping-Pong ball in a T-shirt cannon!"

Simon shoved apples around until he found what he was looking for. It was the perfect size and shape to fit in and then plug up the chute. He yanked it out of the pile by its rubbery stem.

"Grab that handle up there and climb back into the chute," Simon coached Soraiya.

"I'm in," said Soraiya.

"Scoot over," said Simon. "I'm climbing in, too. And I'm bringing my Ping-Pong ball with me."

"What?"

"Sorry. It's how I built an elevator for my Ferris wheel in the library maker space."

Fighting the blast from the fan, Simon grabbed a handle grip, climbed up into the tube, and dragged the round red ball in behind him. He yanked on the stem hard and squeezed the apple into the tube.

When he and it were securely inside, the compressed air did its job and shot everything stuffed into the chute upward. Simon and Soraiya rode the apple ball just like they were riding Simon's Ping-Pong elevator.

Thirty seconds later, they popped out of the trapdoor on the second floor and made a soft, bouncy landing.

"What the—?" said Jack, jumping back.

"We're here to finish our game!" said Simon.

"Who cares? I already finished mine. The face I was

looking for was Philip. The dude with the Abe Lincoln beard. You're back just in time to hear my riddle. My *last* riddle. Then I'm going to win the game and take over Mr. Lemoncello's whole empire."

"Actually," said Soraiya, "this is just the first of several titanium tickets to be—"

"Whatever!" screamed Jack. "The first titanium ticket is going to be mine! Give me my riddle, Philip!"

The face from the Guess Who? game cleared its throat. "Ahem. Two fathers and two sons sat down to eat eggs for breakfast. They ate exactly three eggs. Each person ate only one egg. How?"

Simon recognized the riddle.

It was the same one that Ms. Pulliam had posted on the board in her classroom.

"One of the fathers is also a grandfather," blurted Jack. "His son is the father of the other son."

"Congratulations, JACK," said a soothing voice purring out of the ceiling speakers. "You have successfully completed all eight games. Good luck with the rest of your quest. I hope you make it to the finals."

Jack stared at his tablet screen and waited for the blanks to fill in.

"I gave you that answer!" shouted Simon. "I wrote it on a sticky note in Ms. Pulliam's classroom. You stole my answer."

"Says who?"

"Me!"

"Whatever," said Jack. "It doesn't matter now. All my letters are filled in. . . ."

He looked puzzled.

"Gobs of giggly fun?" he mumbled. "What the heck does that mean?"

Then a light bulb went off over his head.

"Of course! That little kids' board game on the first floor, Giggle Wiggle, the giant caterpillar."

Jack took off running, leaving Pimple Pete standing there, grinning his goofy grin.

"Now we need to finish our game!" Soraiya said to the ceiling.

"Right you are!" said the game show announcer voice. "Resetting the board. Putting fifty seconds back on the clock."

The twenty-four TVs flickered on and off, leaving only the five female characters.

"Okay," said Soraiya. "Is our character black?"

"Yes."

Four of the female faces disappeared.

Only one face remained.

"The answer is Anne," said Soraiya, shaking her head. "The only black woman in the whole game."

"You are correct!" screamed the game show announcer.

"Soraiya?" said the cartoon of Anne.

"Um, yes, Anne?"

"You'll be happy to know that because of the comments, complaints, and concerns from children just like you, future editions of Guess Who? were redesigned to feature a more racially diverse cast of characters."

"Excellent."

"Back to business," said Anne. "Here is your riddle: When things go wrong, what can you always count on?"

Soraiya looked to Simon. "Do you know the answer?"

Simon didn't.

But then he did!

"Your fingers!" shouted Simon. "When things go wrong, you can always count on your fingers."

Bells rang. Trumpets blared. The IPad *DING*ed and one last bubble word zipped across its screen.

CONGRATULATIONS!
13 68

The voice in the ceiling started purring again. "Congratulations, SORAIYA and MARIO, correction, SIMON. You have correctly completed all eight games. Good luck with the rest of your quest. I hope you BOTH make it to the finals."

The C and the G took their places and completed the seventy-six-letter phrase:

GREAT SUCCESS COMES FROM DEDICATION, DOING YOUR BEST, AND, OF COURSE, HAVING GOBS OF GIGGLY FUN!

“You were right all along,” Soraiya told Simon. “You knew exactly what the phrase would say. I slowed us down. We should’ve just gone with it.”

“We’re in this together, Soraiya. We’re a team. We went with the scientific method. It was the, you know, the scientific thing to do.”

Soraiya smiled. “Thanks, Simon. You’re a good friend.”

“You are, too.”

“Wait a second,” said Soraiya, snapping her fingers. “Jack could be right. The titanium ticket might be hidden with Giggle Wiggle. It’s a cute towering caterpillar with tons of hands and feet. Maybe the ticket is in one of its hands!”

“Then why are these sixteen lemon letters glowing?” asked Simon.

He and Soraiya focused on the screen.

G-E-C-E-C-D-E-D-C-D-G-D-C-E-G-G. The letters were all blazing yellow. Then they started blinking.

“It could be a word scramble,” said Simon. “Or a code . . .”

“What words can we make with these sixteen letters?”

Kyle Keeley stepped into the room.

“Yep,” he said, not sounding sick at all. “This is as far as Akimi and I got, too.”

“You’re not sick?” said Simon.

“Not anymore,” said Kyle. “I mean, I was sick to my stomach when I saw how Jack McClintock sabotaged you in that outdoor board game. But we can talk about that later. You two need to get to work. It’s seven-fifty-seven!”

“We only have three minutes!” said Soraiya. “What words can we make with these sixteen letters?”

“Um, egged, edged,” said Simon, even though his mind wasn’t really in the word-generating game.

There was something about the letters that seemed familiar. Something, strangely, that reminded him of his attic and all its recycled and reimagined toys and games.

“Cede, deed, egg,” said Soraiya. “Egg! That’s it, Simon! Dad told me about a game Mr. Lemoncello created like twenty years ago. It’s called the Eggstraordinary Egg Head. There are a dozen plastic eggs in a carton. You fill some with whipped cream. You shuffle them up in the carton, spin the dial, and take turns plucking up an egg and cracking it against your forehead.”

Simon nodded. He was still thinking.

Soraiya was frantically tapping the IPad. “There’s an

antique Egg Head game in the Mr. Lemoncello's Classics section up on the third floor."

"But we're on the first floor."

"I know! That's why we need to hurry, Simon. We're running out of time."

The clock in the atrium started bonging out its hourly melody.

Bing-bong-bing-bong.

Bing-bong-bing-bong.

Soraiya threw up her arms in frustration. "Now we are officially out of time. The clock's about to strike eight."

"Of course!" said Simon.

"Huh?"

The clock chimed the next two lines of its on-the-hour tune.

Bing-bong-bing-bong.

Bing-bong-bing-bong.

"It's a four-note, four-line musical phrase."

He started running.

Out of the Guess Who? exhibit.

Down the nearest staircase.

Soraiya was right behind him.

Simon and Soraiya tore through the first-floor displays and weaved their way back to the atrium.

"That's why Haley and Carolyn were dancing to a song called 'Every Good Boy Deserves Fudge'!" Simon shouted. "That was a clue. That's how you remember the lines of the treble clef in music. E-C-D-G are musical notes. The glowing letters are an anagram, but for music, not a word! E-C-D-G, G-D-E-C, E-D-C-G, G-D-E-C!"

"I have absolutely no idea what you're talking about," said Soraiya.

"The Westminster chimes melody," said Simon, remembering some of the clocks he'd torn apart. "It's what you'd hear ringing out of Big Ben in London!"

As the melody finished, the clock started bonging out the hour just as Simon and Soraiya skidded into the atrium.

"Hurry!" said Soraiya. "There are only seven bell bongs left!"

"No," said Simon, pointing up at the big egg timer. "The game didn't officially start until Mr. Lemoncello tipped over the timer. There's still five minutes or so left. And remember what Mr. Lemoncello said? 'When the clock in the museum's grand hall strikes the hour, pay very close attention. For that is when the big game truly begins!' That was another clue!"

"The big game!" said Soraiya, realizing Simon was right. "The one where we compete to win Mr. Lemoncello's fortune and game-making empire. The championship round of the competition starts when that clock strikes the hour. It starts now."

Simon and Soraiya were standing directly underneath the clock as it continued to mark the eight o'clock hour. The animated wooden figures danced and swirled and juggled. The little Luigi character tossed back his head and laughed. The moon phase dial lit up as it became a smiling man in the moon.

And directly underneath that moon, something silvery, the size of a credit card, slid out of a hidden slot.

"That's it!" shouted Soraiya. "That's the titanium ticket!"

"How do we retrieve it?" Soraiya asked excitedly. "It's at least fifteen feet off the ground!"

"We need to improvise a solution!" said Simon. He looked around the room.

What could they use?

All the ladders from the Chutes and Ladders games had retreated to their standby positions in the basement. There was nothing for Simon to climb on.

Unless . . .

He ran over to the nearest towering column created out of stacked game board boxes. He gave it a shove.

It was on wheels. It could be moved.

Next, he pushed on one of the boxes in the column. It moved, too! It jutted out like a foothold in a rock climbing wall.

If he moved enough boxes in the pillar of cardboard

and staggered their angles as he climbed, he could build a stepladder out of game box lids.

He shoved the column over to the wall so it was standing directly beside the grandfather clock.

"I'm making my own ladder!" he shouted to Soraiya.

"Be careful!" she shouted back as Simon began to scale the box top ledges as if he were scaling a cliff.

"There are five minutes of sand remaining in the two-hour glass," announced the always pleasant prerecorded lady in the ceiling speakers.

"Five minutes left?" said Jack, racing into the atrium. He was holding another controller in his hands. "I heard the clock. I thought the game was—"

He froze when he reached the middle of the open room where the light must've been just right for him to see the glint of something shiny sticking out of a slot in the face of the towering grandfather clock.

"Is that the titanium ticket?"

"Yes, JACK," purred the ceiling lady. "That is the titanium ticket."

Jack's focus whipped over to where Simon was climbing the column of board game boxes.

"This game isn't over yet!" shouted Jack. He jabbed a series of buttons on his controller.

A new mechanical creature wiggled its way into the room. A thirty-foot-tall, upright plastic caterpillar with googly eyes, bright-yellow antennae, and a goofy grin shimmied across the atrium floor. All twenty-four of its

Mickey Mouse–gloved hands were waggling. They'd make a perfect, if unsteady, ladder!

The wiggling giant rocked and twisted its way across the room.

"Attack!" cried Jack.

Simon realized that Jack wasn't going to climb up the caterpillar. He was going to use its swinging hands to try to topple Simon's column of game board boxes. Simon was about to become a plank in a Kooky Kujenga game!

He looked down.

Soraiya wasn't in the atrium!

Where'd she go?

The caterpillar nudged Simon's tower with a line of swaying cartoon hands.

"There are three minutes of sand remaining in the two-hour glass," said the ceiling speakers.

Simon took a deep breath. He wasn't going to let Jack McClintock, or a giant plastic caterpillar, or anybody else, push him around anymore.

He scaled the column, which shook every time the caterpillar's paws smacked into it. He started climbing the stack two and three boxes at a time.

He looked down again.

Now Jack was climbing up the tall caterpillar's limbs like that other Jack climbing his beanstalk. To make his climb easier, he'd switched off the caterpillar's wiggle. Simon's column of boxes was no longer in danger of being knocked down.

Jack was an excellent athlete. In a flash, he was up to the same level as Simon. They were neck and neck.

"Give it up, Skrindle!" shouted Jack. "Nobody wants you to represent Hudson Hills or the factory in the championship round! They want me!"

"There are two minutes of sand remaining in the two-hour glass," said the ceiling speakers.

Suddenly, Simon and Jack froze. They heard the heavy thud of mammoth feet.

Had some kind of giant just entered the atrium?

Both climbers looked down.

Soraiya was back, with a controller in her hands. She was using it to guide Red, the colossal robot from the Rock 'Em Sock 'Em Robots game, over to the base of the grandfather clock.

"Hey!" shouted Jack from his precarious perch. "Those manual controllers are for staff use only!"

Soraiya ignored him and jabbed a complex combination of button bops, the way she'd jabbed them when she played Fourth Knight.

"Turn that caterpillar into a butterfly, Red!" she shouted.

With a mechanical whir, Red led with a strong right hook to one of the bright-green bellies near the bottom of Jack's towering caterpillar.

"Nooooo!" Jack screamed as the teetering caterpillar

creaked and swayed like a tree felled with one mighty blow from an ax. He held on for dear life.

"Tim-berrrrrrr!" shouted Soraiya.

The caterpillar fell sideways. Luckily for Jack, he was hanging on to a hand that wasn't on the side that hit the floor first.

With Jack out of the race, Simon only had to beat the egg timer.

"There is one minute of sand remaining in the two-hour glass," said the ceiling speakers.

Simon quickly scaled his tower's final footholds, pulled open the glass door covering the grandfather clock's elaborate face, reached in, and plucked out the titanium ticket from beneath the smiling moon.

When he did, the tiny little Luigi figurine leapt up and did a backflip.

Balloons fell from the ceiling. Indoor fireworks streaked across the atrium's glass walls. The grandfather clock's chimes started bonging out a new tune—Elton John's triumphant anthem "I'm Still Standing."

"Nooooo!" shouted Jack as he limped out of the room. "Soraiya isn't a staff member! I demand a rematch!"

From his vantage point near the clock, Simon could see Kyle, Akimi, Andrew, Haley, Carolyn, and Piya over on the second-floor balcony. They were all clapping and cheering for him and Soraiya.

Simon scurried down the column of game board boxes and went over to where Soraiya stood beside Red the robot.

He smiled and said, “Thanks!”

“You did it!” shouted Soraiya.

“No, *we* did it!” Simon shouted back. (They had to shout to be heard over all the clanging Elton John bells.)

Simon held out his hand, the one clutching the titanium ticket.

Soraiya took it and raised it high.

The postgame celebration moved into the Dedication Room.

There were balloons and bunting and ice sculptures of famous board game figures. Waiters passed around trays loaded down with all sorts of finger foods, like cheeseburger sliders and ladyfinger cookies. There was fizzy fruit punch, lemon pound cake, lemon bars, lemon cupcakes, and lemon ricotta pancakes—not to mention a fifteen-layer cake with sixteen different flavors of frosting (none of which were lemon).

Soraiya and Simon stood in front of the wall honoring Simon's parents and shook hands with a long line that included just about everybody who lived in Hudson Hills.

"Never knew you had it in you, Simon," said one person.

"You sure showed us!" said another.

"Way to go, honey!" Mr. Mitchell said proudly to his daughter when it was his turn in the receiving line. "You too, Simon. You know, your parents hired me, straight out of high school. They became my mentors."

He shook Simon's hand. "I owe them, big-time. I wish they were here to see all of this!" He swept open his arms to take in the party and the sparkling new building dedicated in the memory of Simon's parents.

"So, when's the next round in the competition?" asked a lady. "When do you two win Mr. Lemoncello's fortune?"

Soraiya laughed. "We don't know. This, after all, is just the first game of the whole tournament."

"That's right," said Kyle Keeley, coming up to shake Simon's and Soraiya's hands. "And, of course, your fiercest competition will come out of Ohio! But today, you are the champions, my friends!"

"Ah, there they are!" Mr. Lemoncello bustled into the crowded room with Dr. Zinchenko. "Sorry to be late. Dr. Z and I had to deal with a last-minute complaint from Jack McClintock. He said that you, Soraiya, manually operated one of our robotic exhibit pieces?"

"Yes, sir. It was an emergency."

"Which is why we want to present you with this medal to go with your titanium ticket," said Dr. Zinchenko as she draped the medal's purple ribbon over Soraiya's head.

Soraiya read what was emblazoned on the medallion: "Safety First!"

"That's my girl!" boomed Mr. Mitchell. "But, uh,

speaking of safety, I'm afraid, sir, we need to hire a new director of security. Buck McClintock just quit. Then he wrote a bunch of nasty stuff on Twitter about you and me and pasted in some of the ruder emoji. . . . I don't even know what this one means. . . ."

"Well," said Mr. Lemoncello, "I'm sorry to lose him. No, wait. I'm not. I was thinking about my keys. I was sorry to lose those. . . ."

Just then, Mr. Raymo, the chief imagineer, came into the Dedication Room.

Simon's grandparents were with him.

Simon braced himself. He knew his grandfather was going to yell at him. But then his grandmother gave him a wink and a thumbs-up.

Simon's grandfather walked up to the memorial wall and rubbed the engraved letters of his son's and daughter-in-law's names.

Everyone else in the room quit talking.

Mr. Lemoncello stood ramrod stiff so his banana shoes wouldn't accidentally burp-squeak.

"You know," Simon's grandfather said, without turning around, "I had forgotten that Steve met Sally right here, working at the factory. Fortunately, just about thirty minutes ago, my wife was able to remind me, in no uncertain terms, that some of the best things in our lives came to us courtesy of Mr. Luigi L. Lemoncello. My son's beautiful and brainy wife. Their beautiful and brainy son."

He turned around.

"I'm sorry, Simon. Your grandmother is right. Life is for living. Sure, you need to work hard, but you ought to have some fun while you're doing it, too."

He opened his arms.

Simon ran into them.

"I'm so proud of you, Simon."

Finally, Grandpa Sam broke out of the hug and walked over to Mr. Lemoncello.

"Now then," he said, "if my grandson and his friend Soraiya here are really going to take over your factory . . ."

"They might," said Mr. Lemoncello, bouncing on his heels. "We're already planning a few more competitions in our tournament to determine my successor."

"Well," said Grandpa Sam, "whoever wins, they should have this. I found it with Steve's things, years ago. Probably should've shared it with you back then, but, well . . . here."

He handed Mr. Lemoncello a rolled-up tube of engineering drawings.

"Steve thought you ought to reconfigure your plastic mold injector. Since heat rises, it'd be more energy efficient if the heating tube was horizontal instead of vertical. That way, both ends would be the same temperature and you'd get even melting."

Mr. Lemoncello beamed. "Like father, like son."

Grandpa Sam looked confused. Simon smiled. He realized where he got his puzzle-solving skills: from his mom and dad.

Mr. Lemoncello took the plans from Grandpa Sam.

"I'll be sure to pass this on to whoever inherits my empire."

"You're really giving it all away?" asked Grandpa Sam.

"Oh, yes indeedy. Some young puzzle solver—maybe someone right here in this very room or someone back home in Ohio or someone somewhere I haven't even imagined—will, one day, inherit everything that I have spent my entire life building. But for now, we play on!"

"That's right," said Simon with a wink to Soraiya. "This game has just begun!"

ARE THE GAMES OVER?

Of course not! The names of over six dozen real board games, past and present, have been sprinkled into the text of this book.

How many can you find?

Send your answer to author@ChrisGrabenstein.com. One winner, selected on August 25, 2021, from all the entries listing the most board games, will win a very cool prize. (Well, not as cool as inheriting Mr. Lemoncello's entire empire, but cool!)

THANK YOU!

So many people have helped Mr. Lemoncello since his very first book came out, it's almost impossible to thank all of them.

But I'll try!

First and foremost, thank you to my extremely talented, patient, and funny wife, J.J. She's not only my amazing coauthor on *Shine!* but the first editor of everything I write, including all five Lemoncello books.

Speaking of editors, the fantabulous Shana Corey and I have now done ten books together (with more to come!). She is amazingly insightful and knows how to make everything she touches better. She is ably assisted—and so am I—by Polo Orozco (when he's not too busy managing security for Mr. Lemoncello's Imagination Factory, that is).

I'd also like to thank Maria Modugno, editor of my picture book *No More Naps!,* because you don't get to thank people in the back of picture books.

Big thanks to my longtime literary agent, Eric Myers, who takes care of all the serious stuff so that I can focus on the silly stuff.

Many thanks for the support and guidance from all of Mr. Lemoncello's wondermous friends at Random House Children's Books: John Adamo, Kerri Benvenuto, Julianne Conlon, Janet Foley, Judith Haut, Kate Keating, Jules Kelly, Gillian Levinson, Mallory Loehr, Barbara Marcus, Kelly McGauley, Michelle Nagler, and Janine Perez.

Mr. Lemoncello's brand-new cover look was created by James Lancett. Thanks to him and Michelle Cunningham, Katrina Damkoehler, Stephanie Moss, Trish Parcell, Martha Rago, April Ward, and everybody in the Random House Children's Books art department for making Luigi look so good.

An author is just one part of the team that makes a book. Ginormous thanks to more folks at Random House:

Copyediting: Barbara Bakowski, Heather Hughes, and Alison Kolani

Production: Shameiza Ally and Tim Terhune

Publicity: Dominique Cimina, Noreen Herits, and Lili Feinberg

School and library marketing: Shaughnessy Miller, Emily Petrick, Kristin Schulz, and Adrienne Waintraub

Sales (the crew that gets the right books into the right kids' hands): Suzanne Archer, Amanda Auch, Emily Bruce, Gretchen Chapman, Brenda Conway, Dandy Conway, Whitney Conyers, Stephanie Davey, Jenelle Davis, Nic DuFort, Cletus Durkin, Felicia Frazier, Stella Galatis, Alex Gottlieb, Becky Green, Susan Hecht, Christina Jeffries, Kimberly Langus, Katie Lenox, Ruth Liebmann, Lauren

Mackey, Cindy Mapp, Dennis McLaughlin, Deanna Meyerhoff, Carol Monteiro, Tim Mooney, Stacey Pyle, Michele Sadler, Mark Santella, William Steedman, Ceara Steffan, Kate Sullivan, and Richard Vallejo.

Finally, thank you once again to all the teachers, librarians, parents, and grandparents who have introduced Mr. Lemoncello to millions of children all over the world! Thank you, thank you, thank you!

CHRIS GRABENSTEIN

is the *New York Times* bestselling author of the hilarious and critically acclaimed Mr. Lemoncello's Library and Welcome to Wonderland series, *The Island of Dr. Libris*, *Shine!* (coauthored with J.J. Grabenstein), and many other books, as well as the coauthor of numerous page-turners with James Patterson, including *Katt vs. Dogg* and the Treasure Hunters and Max Einstein series. Chris lives in New York City with his wife, J.J. Visit ChrisGrabenstein.com for trailers, bonus puzzles, and more. Look for Chris's next book, *The Smartest Kid in the Universe*, coming soon!

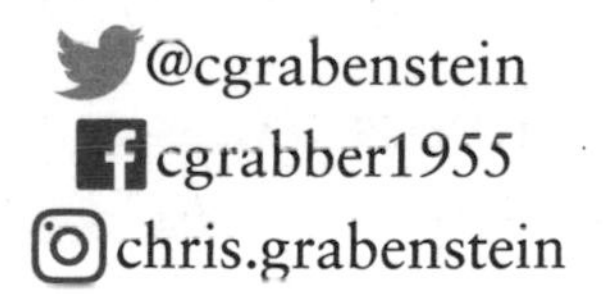

FAVORITES BY CHRIS GRABENSTEIN

The Island of Dr. Libris
Shine! (coauthored with J.J. Grabenstein)

THE MR. LEMONCELLO'S LIBRARY SERIES

Escape from Mr. Lemoncello's Library
Mr. Lemoncello's Library Olympics
Mr. Lemoncello's Great Library Race
Mr. Lemoncello's All-Star Breakout Game
Mr. Lemoncello and the Titanium Ticket

THE WELCOME TO WONDERLAND SERIES

Home Sweet Motel
Beach Party Surf Monkey
Sandapalooza Shake-Up
Beach Battle Blowout

THE HAUNTED MYSTERY SERIES

The Crossroads
The Demons' Door
The Zombie Awakening
The Black Heart Crypt

COAUTHORED WITH JAMES PATTERSON

The House of Robots series
The I Funny series
The Jacky Ha-Ha series
Katt vs. Dogg
The Max Einstein series
Pottymouth and Stoopid
The Treasure Hunters series
Word of Mouse